01/21

$ 3.00

D0049517

TESS GALLAGHER

At the Owl Woman Saloon

SCRIBNER

SCRIBNER
1230 Avenue of the Americas
New York, NY 10020

SCRIBNER and design are trademarks of
Simon & Schuster Inc.

Designed by Brooke Zimmer
Set in Dante Monotype
Manufactured in the United States of America

3 5 7 9 10 8 6 4 2

Library of Congress Cataloging-in-Publication Data

Gallagher, Tess.
At the Owl Woman Saloon / Tess Gallagher.
p. cm.
I. Title.
PS3557. A41156A92   1997
813´.54—dc21   97-1399
CIP

ISBN 0-684-82693-3

See page 233 for text credits.

for Josie Gray and for Dorothy Catlett—
my wings.
And for Ray—
at sky

Acknowledgments

Many stories in this collection, some in different form, originally appeared in the following publications:

Atlantic Monthly ("The Poetry Baron"), *Five Points* ("A Glimpse of the Buddha" and "To Dream of Bears"), *Glimmer Train* ("Mr. Woodriff's Neckties"), *Indiana Review* ("Venison Pie"), *Kenyon Review* ("My Gun"), *Michigan Quarterly Review* ("The Mother Thief"), *The Paris Review* ("The Leper"), *Ploughshares* ("Creatures" and "Coming and Going"), *Northwest Review* ("She Who Is Untouched by Fire"), *Story* ("A Box of Rocks"), *Sycamore Review* ("Rain Flooding Your Campfire"), and *Zyzzyva* ("I Got a Guy Once").

I would like to thank the Lyndhurst Foundation for the grant which allowed me time to write these stories. I give special thanks to Dorothy Catlett, who gave, in fact and spirit, far beyond the call of duty in her unfailing daily contributions to this book. Josie Gray listened to me as I read the entire book aloud, and I thank him for that, and for just plain standing behind and beside me. I give thanks for the gifts of listening and faith I received from Judy Martin, Teresa Olson, Alfredo Arreguin, Lesley Arreguin and Susan Lytle, Rijl and Stephanie Barber, Margaret Matthieu, Dr. Robert Marks, Morris and Larri Ann Bond, Georgia Bond, Frank Barhydt, Alice Derry, Karen Whalley, Bill and Pat McDowell, Jay Hereford, Laurie Bond, Drago Stambuk, Linda Stern, Joe Denhart, Steve Mishko, Greg Simon, Harold and Lynne Schweizer, and especially Bill Stull and Maureen Carroll. Dick Catlett did research for me on saloons in the West, for which I am especially thankful. I thank all the editors who took stories for magazines, but especially Howard Junker and Richard Ford, who made special contributions to the final composition of the stories they chose, "I Got a Guy Once" and "Coming and Going," respectively. To Leigh Haber, my editor, I give thanks for her acute and deep-hearted editing. I am fortunate and grateful for the ongoing support of my longtime agent, Amanda Urban. Finally, I thank Ray, always Ray.

Contents

SALON *(Fr.—Hall) 1: an apartment for the reception of guests*
2: a periodic gathering, usually at the home of a distinguished woman, of persons of note in artistic, literary, or political circles
3: a hall in which works of art are displayed

SALOON *(Americanism) misspelling of the above. A public house, a barroom, a drinking place*
—Consolidated Webster 1957

At the
Owl Woman
Saloon

*It was at the heart of the old western saloon that it
was womanless . . .*

The

Red

Ensign

The white-haired man at the Owl Woman Salon leans his head into the sink to the left of mine. I'm thinking MAN the way Ms. Piggy says CHOC-O-LATE. He doesn't seem to care he's the only male person in the salon. Plus, he looks nothing like the unisex veterans migrated from L.A. to this recalcitrant little corner, where women believe fraternizing with men while getting their hair done is a barbarism we shouldn't import.

Looking at him from the side, one death mask to another, his head is handsome the way even brooding men in Bergman movies can be—the disposition a little spoiled, but overlaid with so much determination to overcome this basic fault that, instead of being spoiled and brooding, you feel such men are positively optimistic.

Why, if your ship was sinking, you would jump right into their glum little lifeboat.

I should mention right here that when my head is under running water I have a persistent and unreasonable fear of drowning. At the hairdresser's this always makes for interludes of controlled hysteria and miraculous escape, though I have never let on to Jenny, who owns the salon. I can trace this fear all the way back to the drowning of my cousin Richie, when I was eight. But that doesn't stop the fear. If you want to know what I look like with my head under water, think of a child who's just bitten down on a raw gooseberry.

Both our heads, mine and this man's, are sinking into the porcelain. Jenny's sister, Becky, is working over the old gent, lathering him up. He has a crown of foamy white curls. Jenny pays him no mind. She's telling me about a teenage customer from the day before.

"This little bit of stuff won't lean back to the sink and I can't figure it. That's when I discover two iguanas clutched to her back, inside her T-shirt. 'Look, these iguanas gotta go,' I say, 'or just take your head somewheres else.' "

Jenny is into her customers, but she has limits. "Give me my little blue-haired ladies any day," she says. "I've been asking how their husbands courted. They love to talk about it. You just won't hear stories like theirs these days. I mean, men were persistent. One of these guys took three refusals before he finally got the woman of his dreams to go to a picnic. Then his luck changes. It rains and they end up spending the day in his car. 'Lucky thing,' my client says, 'the car had a radio.' Then she goes, 'Ho, ho, ho!' " Jenny is giggling like an early-morning robin.

Meanwhile Becky is talking to the man like he's a

regular. "Frank," she says, "did you turn your garden plot?"

"Too darn wet," Frank says. "Grass over my boot tops."

This starts me telling Jenny about my sweet peas, ordered all the way from England. Before summer is out, I'll have bouquets stationed at every workstand. I recite their names like ice-cream flavors, they are that delicious. "Blue Danube," I say. "Firecrest, Gypsy Queen, Lilac Silk, Orange Dragon, and Red Ensign." I emphasize the trouble I've taken, scoring each with a knife to ensure every water-soaked seed is going to sprout.

"I always beat the crowd with sweet peas," the head named Frank says. "I start in January, dig my row down in a V. I put in seed, then sprinkle dirt over."

He's looking at the ceiling. I'm looking there too. The hot water is rushing over both our heads from time to time, and I'm sucking in little breaths of petrified air between bursts of water to calm myself. Meanwhile, he's gassing on.

"When the sprout shoves up, I throw on more dirt to barely cover it," he says. His description is making me claustrophobic. I feel like this small, light-starved seed with dirt raining down on my face every time I make it to the surface.

"I coax it along," he says. "When everyone else is just putting in seed, my sweet peas are halfway to my knees." Becky sees Frank has leaped the imaginary boundary between customers and engaged my attention.

"Frank's an amazing gardener," she says.

"Don't cover them too much or they get discouraged and rot," Frank says. By now I am trying to hold my breath inside my chest like a gigantic oxygen capsule out of which I could subsist even at the earth's molten core.

"Frank's camellia bushes were loaded this year," Becky says. Behind her a woman, helmeted with rows of white spring-loaded curlers, catches my attention. I take a deep breath from my interior supply. The outside air is smarting with nose-hating perm solution. The woman raises her *Star,* the one I've already read, about how O. J. Simpson has hidden his 6.5 million on the Isle of Man.

I'm on my way to hating this guy Frank. Loaded camellia bushes is a step too far. Jack-in-the-beanstalk sweet peas? No, thanks—I'd rather drown and be snacked on by sharks than climb into this man's lifeboat. I waste just enough oxygen to say, as a kind of advance warning system, "My white camellias turned brown. They froze," I add with chilly emphasis.

"That's not freeze. That's rain rust," he says.

I've never heard of rain rust and don't intend to go into it. Jenny has me sitting up and is battering my head with a towel to get my hair ready to blow-dry. The tap is off. Oxygen, tainted with perm fumes, is flowing freely again through my body. I am giddy with survival.

"Rain turns white camellias brown," the expert says. I glance over and see that, with his white curls rinsed down the sink, he has that used-car-salesman veneer, wet hair rat-slicked to his skull.

"I came here at nineteen from Aberdeen and learned to build boats in the shipyard," he says, as if this will get things on track. "But flowers, they're my real occupation." Even if he built his own lifeboat, fitted it with a full working bar, a CB radio and fishing poles, I would not climb into it. *Especially* if he built it.

Just then *another* man walks into the Owl Woman. The lady behind the *Star* peers out. She's probably incredulous at this double trespass. *Two men* in the Owl Woman Salon! I attribute it to Jenny's recent ill-considered, but financially prudent, decision to take "walk-ins." Are these guys illiterate or what? *"Owl Woman Salon,"* the sign says. Did they think it said "Owl Woman SALOON"? I am thinking: saloon or salon—you walk in one way and come out another, when the second man sits down before the sink on the other side of me.

"Joe!" Frank says, as if he's been at sea for weeks and just hit harbor. He reaches across me, dripping water, to shake hands with the new man. "This here's one of my shooters," Frank says, introducing me to this lanky old bird in suspenders. Before Joe can say a word, the beautician tending him has his head back and he's squinting toward the ceiling. I don't have the faintest idea what a "shooter" is. I would rather be home shaking fish fertilizer down on my sweet peas.

"Have you ever seen a twenty-one-gun salute?" Frank asks. Now that's conversation, I'd say. But I don't say a word—even though I have now stockpiled enough oxygen to recite "In Praise of Limestone," if anyone cared to listen, which they usually don't, except here at the Owl Woman. But then many things get heard here, like Lolly Davis's recipe for Baked Beans with Chutney and the songs Jella Barkley sang at Girl Scouts in 1953.

I'm taking my first fully collected look at Mr. Know-it-all and am surprised to see he is more like a well-aged Gérard Depardieu than a Bergman type. He has that flared-nostril look that is funny and sexy at the same time. Still, this whole encounter has the sinking prospect of a bad wedding night in County Leitrim. It's enough to cause me to take refuge in my Irish gene pool—women able and ready for anything: potato-peel soup, hefting turf in the rain, fiddles lashing away into the dawn. In honor of them I could stuff my fear of drowning in order to carry the slumped and drunken form of my supposed mate across the Shannon to a little pub, hoping to revive him with half a dozen pints. Later there would at least be a good story: "Ah, the swift and terrible currents of the Shannon!" I could embellish the offering with beckoning flutes and fish weaving through my thighs.

Have I ever seen a 21-gun salute?

"Only at funerals on TV," I tell Frank. By then Jenny is on me with the dryer, and the closest thing I've felt in months to a Mediterranean breeze is blowing into the sexy space between my hair and the back of my neck.

"Joe here's in the firing party, one of our seven," Frank persists, over the roar of the dryer. "We serve at all the VFW burials, when requested. I'm the escort commander. I position the party so it faces toward Canada. Then I give my commands." The din of the hair dryer is adding a warplane intensity to this exchange. I shout, in what I imagine is a brave voice, "Are those real bullets in your rifles?"

"Blank cartridges only," Frank says. "We load with the muzzle at a forty-five-degree angle, then fire at exactly the interval it takes to unload and reload a musket. That's where the timing developed, back in musket times. We're using the M-One Garand. You ever seen a twenty-one-gun salute? You might like to. Joe here goes to our practices. But we don't wear our uniforms at practice."

Then the water-thrashed voice of Joe, like a genie inside a waterfall, says, "Just check the paper. When you see a VFW died, we'll likely be there."

"It goes like this," Frank says. "The right cheeks of my men are pressed against the stocks of their rifles." He is sighting along his arm straight into the courthouse across the street. "The left eye is shut, the right eye fixed over the rear sight. They unlock their rifles. I command: 'Ready. Aim.' Just a pause, then: 'FIRE!' Seven fingers are squeezing seven triggers. KER-BLAM! They lower to the reload position. I repeat these commands twice more and that's your twenty-one. It's an occasion you don't want to miss," Frank says.

There are comb tracks through his spectacularly white hair and he is at least twenty-five years older than me. Until now I have never considered that, in passing off earth, a 21-gun salute was something I might regret never having experienced. Still, something has thrilled me, I admit, when this man says, "Fire!" How many women have had 21-gun salutes? I wonder, but assume we're catching up there too, as in everything. If I am sure of anything on earth, it's that I will never be given a 21-gun salute.

Jenny, dryer at full speed, is bearing down on me again like a kamikaze. She pulls out of her dive somewhere above my left eyebrow just as Becky unfurls the peach-colored cape from Frank's shoulders. He gets up a little stiffly and pulls on his jacket.

"See you, Joe," he says.

Does the man so much as glance at me or say good-bye? He pays at the counter across the room and wafts out the door before I've begun to realize this obviously amazing gentleman is possibly walking out of my life forever, taking with him all his garden know-how, his sixty-five years of life savvy, not to mention nightlong war stories full of waste and shame, tinged with occasional valor. He is not like any of the forty-year-olds I've been dating since my divorce, who want to talk about their unmet needs in their last marriage, or how they've had to borrow on their retirement portfolios to make their child-support payments.

The door to the Owl Woman opens and shuts. Frank

pauses to read the verse from the Owl Woman's song on the door, which I would gladly have recited to him:

> *In the great night my heart will go out,*
> *Toward me the darkness comes rattling,*
> *In the great night my heart will go out.**

I wonder whether, like Jenny, who chose the name "Owl Woman" for her salon, Frank believes in spirits. Are those blank cartridges fired only for the benefit of the living to honor the dead? Maybe the dead line up along the cliff with their backs to Canada when the shooters arrive, so when the guns go off they can slap each other on the shoulders or hug each other while real imaginary bullets pass through them, confirming their miraculous escape from the living. Or maybe, as Owl Woman—the great Papago healer—believed, the spirits are holding in close to their graves during the daylight, just milling around, singing and telling stories, oblivious to everything but spirit-things, waiting to go forth powerfully at night.

I started coming to the Owl Woman just to get my hair done. But maybe because I'm always dueling with the fates to keep from drowning, I see spirits here. They are moving around in the daytime. They speak to each other, appear and disappear. Speak or are silent. I try to get as close as possible to them in this walking-around life—without leaving the daylight. I'm probably one of them. That's why I believe there is as much *unseen* world around me as there is *seen*. At the Owl Woman I feel this, am able to admit it. I suppose, if Frank is a regular, Jenny has been talking to him about such things.

*Tohono O'odham: Owl Woman. Her Spanish name was Juana Maxwell. From "Healing Songs," translated by Frances Densmore, in *Poetry of the American West,* edited by Allison Hawthorn Deming, (New York: Columbia University Press, 1996).

Frank, of the 21-gun salute, walks past the plate-glass window, head up, shoulders at attention. *The Red Ensign,* I think. Suddenly I know I would follow him anywhere. Up the beaches at Normandy. Across the Alps in my bedroom slippers. I have discharged all my guns—rendered my ship, my fort, my battery defenseless. I wouldn't care if I'd met him in the last ten minutes of his life, as maybe I have. I'm prepared to plant sweet peas in January. Ready to discover rain rust and how to stop it, or that it just has to be lived with, like we do the rain. We are drifting away in the lifeboat. The Red Ensign is at the helm.

The men who bellied up to the bar and acquired calluses on their elbows by prolonged and heavy leaning on the counter did not patronize the saloon simply for its alcoholic refreshments. Many old habitués pointed out repeatedly that if a fellow wanted to hear the owl hoot, it would have been more effective and a lot cheaper to buy himself a gallon of barrelhouse whiskey and retire to his dugout or bunkhouse to work himself up for his case of jimjams. Men, however, did not drink alone, and they did not drink at home. Westerners were a gregarious lot. They needed each other's company, even if only to pick a fight.

I

Got

a

Guy

Once

Danny Gunnerson's mailbox had a serious look, like it could handle any kind of news. Someone had even painted it black, for good measure. I glanced inside to make sure the mail hadn't come, then sat down on the bumper of a blue jeep parked just off the main road. The sun was pushing through for the usual early-afternoon break in the overcast, and I'd started to sweat in my flannel shirt.

Danny owed me what was, in those days, a lot of money—about three thousand dollars. He probably owed others, which accounted for his telling everyone he was going bankrupt long before it happened. At first Danny had told me he wasn't getting checks, period. They just weren't hitting his mailbox. "The mill has quit paying," he kept telling us. "They're just stacking logs in the yard. If Japan doesn't fork over, nobody gets paid." I tried, but couldn't figure it. I knew the same company was paying boys in other outfits every two weeks.

He'd been stringing us along like a clothesline to China, and the poor prospects of timber cutting meant he could get away with it. Meanwhile, when I'd missed child-support payments, my ex-wife had turned collection over to the state. I'd moved a renter into my house as a stopgap for some kind of steady income. The state had threatened to confiscate my pickup, plus my land and everything on it, if I didn't pay up. The pickup they could have. I had even put a sign on it to warn people of its value: NOT A PIECE OF JUNK. GENUINE ARTIFACT OF SPOTTED OWL ERA. I thought tourists would appreciate the local color, since tourists were what we had of light industry these days.

But there had to be an end to Danny's stringing us along. So I worked out which day the check should be delivered to his place, then drove there to sit, big as a jay-bird, near his mailbox.

Gunnerson had one of those stump ranches halfway up Lost Mountain. A wooden boat had dead-ended practically on his doorstep. Marooned near a trailer house was a lime-green sofa, minus its cushions. Half a dozen fat white geese were pulling tufts of sick-looking yellow grass between rusted vehicles and appliances.

It was peaceful to lean against the jeep with the sun hazing through, and I got to thinking about the mail carrier who'd be coming along anytime now. I knew Joe Cooper had this route, because my Aunt Trina lived up the road, and she was always telling me things Joe told her. He was an awful gossip and lady's man. I'd known Joe when he'd been a logger, back when, as they say, the getting was good—long before work in the woods got scarce, with government lands slammed shut to logging. Private timber had been coming down so fast lately that deer were sleeping on our front porches, and a cougar had snapped up a Pomeranian from a backyard near Morse Creek.

Joe hadn't quit logging because of any special eye to the future. Short and simple, he'd developed an honest bad back, like a lot of middle-aged loggers. Then he'd started having some near misses—snags crashing down at his elbow, saws jamming in the butts of trees—things that happen one time or another to anyone who stays long enough with the timber. But Joe read the writing on the wall, while the rest of us just kept getting up with the dawn, hoping for the next stand of timber to cut, even if it turned out to be smack against a playground full of kids.

"How you doing, Billy?" Joe called to me as he pulled up in front of Danny's mailbox. He leaned out the window of his snub-nosed jeep, opened the black mailbox, and, like he was sliding some awful dish into an oven, pushed Gunnerson's mail inside.

"I'm fit as a fiddle in a hailstorm," I said, and went over to Joe.

We shot the breeze and Joe allowed as how he could get me on with the postal service anytime I wanted to pack it in with logging. "Too dangerous," I said. "You think I don't read about those wacko postal workers who blitz their co-workers and innocent P.O. box owners to bejesus with AK-forty-sevens? And what about mail bombs? Hazardous duty, I'd say."

"That's what a regular paycheck will do for you," Joe said. "Fearless, I'm simply fearless." But he grinned in a way that said he missed the old sawdust edge a little. He knew I'd been a gyppo logger for over thirty years and regular paychecks are just a dirty rumor to a gyppo.

"There's nothing I like better than to be in timber," I said. "I'm going to last it out until my tailbone drags the ground like a praying mantis." We had a good laugh on that one. The way he enjoyed my stubbornness let me know he envied me for staying with what I loved. He understood how, with hardly a heartbeat between, a logger can love trees and love to cut them, too.

Once Joe was out of sight, I stepped to the mailbox and reached in. I knew Gunnerson or someone must be home, because wood smoke was sifting from the chimney, one of those slow greenwood fires people in these parts light in the spring to shove back the damp. His yellow pickup, a real beater, was parked in the turnaround. It occurred to me Danny might even be watching through the window, so I tried to be quick. I shuffled the mail like it was a stacked deck and I was hunting the fifth ace. It was there, too. I brought the envelope with the return address from "Jansik, Inc." to the top.

This company had been buying logs as fast as we could lay down trees, then selling them to Japan. One of the longshoremen I knew told me the trees were being used in Japan to make forms for pouring concrete in high-rises. Then, he said, the wood was tossed. I hated to think of such good wood scummed with concrete and lost to a scrap heap. It hurt me, hearing about waste I couldn't stop.

I let the Jansik envelope ride the pile—mainly bills, along with a tools catalog and some coupon packets. Then I knocked the mud off my caulks on the bumper of the jeep and headed for Gunnerson's house. I braved it right through the middle of the geese, hissing when they hissed at me. I must have been convincing because they reared their heads back on their slick cobra-sized necks, then waddled to the side of the house. On the porch there was a kid's trike beside a refrigerator with the door ajar. Pulpy apples and limp celery stalks were sinking through the racks. I felt for Gunnerson. The dead food in his recently disabled refrigerator reminded me he had a family to support, same as me. But he was getting his checks. It was an important difference, and why I was standing on his porch with his mail in my hands.

I gave the front door a good hard-knuckle rap and tried to look in through the frosted glass. Suddenly I was nose to nose with Danny. Before he could say a thing, I handed him the mail, check envelope on top.

"What do you know about that!" I said. "Jansik paid today."

Danny looked like he wished he was anywhere but there holding his mail. I'd worked for him many a time before this. He was a personable enough guy. Could talk you into anything in the way of timber cutting, slash clearing, or snagging a unit, once a cut was finished. I had climbed ridges a mountain goat would have balked at, in order to cut timber for Danny Gunnerson. When the pressure was on to get logs out before closures of one sort and another, I had even cut in windstorms, one of the dumbest things an experienced faller can do. So I'm saying I had put myself out for this guy, and I wasn't ashamed to be standing there on his porch, asking for pay I deserved.

"Probably more excuses," Danny said, glancing at the envelope he'd been expecting all along. "Come in, Billy, come in," he said, and stepped back so I could see into the rooms. The place was a shambles and his wife was still in her robe, so I stayed on the porch. Danny left the door ajar while he went over to a little piled-up table in one corner that served as a desk and brought back what I hoped was a checkbook. He took the Jansik envelope and tore it open. He examined the check and groaned. "I can't believe these jackasses, shorting me like this," he said. "I can let you have three hundred," he told me when he looked up. "That's the best I can do." He made it seem a stretch. "Surely they'll pay the lot in a couple of weeks."

"Surely," I said. He found a pen on the TV and made out a check, leaning over a bronzed clock with its exhausted Indian rider. Then he folded the check in half and handed it to me like it was some kind of secret. It hit me that this was exactly what he intended. I wasn't to let on to the others at the job that I'd gotten paid even a fraction of what I was owed.

"Jake and Paul will be glad to hear the payload came in," I said, and unfolded the check to make sure I wouldn't get down the road to find he hadn't signed it. I looked up as his expression fell, then stuck the check in my shirt pocket and stepped off the porch toward my pickup.

Before the day was out, I made sure my partners got around to Danny's for their shares. In no time, I was able to have my phone turned on and to buy lumber for the outhouse I was hammering together back of what I called my hovel. Fifteen years earlier, I'd built an A-frame on my acreage, complete with a beautiful stone fireplace that a logger-turned-stonemason had run twenty-six feet to the pitch of my roof. It was a monument, that fireplace. I'd packed the stones off a mountaintop myself, a few at a time in my saddlebags. Heather stone it's called, because it's found on ridges above the timberline in patches of heather.

Now another guy, a renter, a man who'd never set eyes on heather stone atop a ridge, was warming his toes at my fireplace. His kids, from various marriages and byways of desire, were scraping crayons down my walls, and his current girlfriend was burning Spam in my skillet. But what could I say? Hey, he paid his rent.

A month back I'd made this retreat to the hovel, which I'd used as a bunkhouse during elk-hunting season. It had come in handy of late as a fall-back position when I'd had to rent my house. Having been run out of house and home, needless to say, it did not sit well when, two weeks after my mailbox visit, Danny came to us hangdog and confessed he was now truly and irreversibly bankrupt. He threw himself on our mercy. Said if we would just cut this one last section, he could maybe sell the logs for lumber to a guy he knew, then put his machinery up for sale. He promised to split the take between us and his other creditors. We knew it was one more promise he was unlikely to keep.

That very day we gathered our gear, took one last look at our spar tree, which was as good as they come—straight and well-rooted—and which we hated to leave, maybe for its resemblance to our own stripped-down lives. It was next to abandoning a brother, to walk off from that spar. But we took our saws, wedges, and falling axes and we walked out of there.

Imagine our surprise three days later when Joe Cooper stopped in at the coffee shop to tell us Danny was still in business, floating home-free on a gang of greenhorns. Naturally the new gang had been promised big pay. The truth would only hit them a couple of weeks later.

I didn't say anything to Joe when he told us this. But I had an image at the back of my mind of that great fir spar bouncing up as it fell, then rebounding several times before it settled in its lay. If the spar goes, that's it. There'd be a shutdown and a good while before another could be rigged and put into use. The thought did not let me rest.

It occurred to me I would even be doing this virgin crew a favor, saving them from putting in so much as another day's work for which they would certainly never see pay.

IN OVER thirty years of falling I had cut trees in all conditions and weather, including snow up to my nostrils, but I had never cut a tree at night. Luckily there was a bloated moon above the ridge. I was amazingly calm and not the least bit at odds with Danny as I hefted my chain saw from the pickup. I felt that all the worn-out, misused loggers, past and present, were somehow with me. Not that this would truly put right the situation between piecemeal thieves like Danny and honest, hardworking folk like Jake, Paul, and myself. The damage was too extensive and ongoing to kid myself about that. But at least this was some show of spirit.

In my twenties I'd logged with a Swede who had said, "Better to be a tiger for one day than a sheep for a thousand." It seemed, at the time, a fairly dangerous idea. Some twenty-five years had passed. I had been a sheep a long time, had gotten comfortable in my woolly ways. But the Swede's words came back to me, there on that mountainside.

In the moonlight the spar looked silver. The block, which is used like a pulley to run cable out from it to yard in each log, was dangling at the tree's stripped crown. Guy wires were stretched to stumps. Before I could bring the block down, I would have to drop these cables. They were fastened to the stumps with railroad spikes, and I used a crowbar to pry the spikes loose. Then I cranked my saw into the tree itself.

That sound of a chain saw in moonlight—I hadn't been ready for that. It made such a raw snarl that I drew the saw blade out of the cut and throttled back. Then silence dropped over me—the velvety, deep quiet of clear-cut, and above that, of trees still growing, untouched high on the ridge. It was a fresh, unwearied silence that probably belongs to the instant before the world was born. The moon seemed to look down at me and to make a great show of itself in all the blue-blackness of sky around it. I felt watched as I cranked the saw again and stepped to the spar.

I set a cut into the base, two feet from the ground. When a pull of air hit the saw, I yanked it out, just as the tree began to hinge from the stump and break into its fall. The spar gave way in slow motion. Its falling seemed so outside time that I was glad to see it finally reach the ground. On impact there was a brittle sound of machinery and I could make out the yarder crushed as easily as a beer can under the trunk.

Just as the spar rebounded I glimpsed something live making a run from the clearing. It was the size of a large dog. A cougar, I guessed, probably displaced by the recent havoc we'd wreaked on that hillside. "It's all over, here," I shouted, my voice coming back to me with too much importance. "Don't you worry," I called into the night. I was speaking to the cougar, but also to the trees, and to the stare-down moon that was shining over what I had just done.

After the spar settled, I went over and ran my hand the length of it, right up to the block, past the stove-in yarder, its snapped wires gone slack. The tree still had plenty of quiver, and I felt sorry all over again to put to waste such a perfectly good spar. At the same time a giddy lightness came over me. I felt like a man with cougar in his veins. I could have clawed my way up a hemlock or skimmed five miles at a bound. It was energy I couldn't account for. Sheep energy, built up for years, working on and off for Danny Gunnerson and the like.

Standing there in moonlight, next to kinked iron and that downed spar, I felt that, at least for those moments, there was something peaceful in having called a line on what you were willing to put up with. Pride is an awful engine, mind you. I had been raised to keep a clear heart, not to do wrong to anyone, and if anyone asked me today, I would stand by that view of life. I would not bother to argue for rightness in what I'd just done, and done out of the usual misbegotten notions that add ruin to ruin in the world. No, this night's work was somewhere out there with cougars and bobcats, with instincts we pledge to mostly overcome. But I figured, right or wrong, that for all the daylight I'd given up to Danny Gunnerson in good faith, I had one such night coming. My mind seemed eerily far-reaching, like that moon-washed night. If an army of Danny Gunnersons were to line up in my future, I hoped maybe I'd walk away with a little more backbone for having taken that spar down, wrongheaded as it was.

The moon was sinking fast by the time I'd finished dropping the block and dragged it a hundred yards into the brush. I piled limbs and salal over it, then went back to the clearing for my saw. The spar was white as a tusk, right where I'd left it, resting on the yarder. I looked toward the edge of the clearing and thought I caught a glimmer of the cranked-up, mad-to-the-core night eyes of a cougar.

I let a day pass, but I couldn't keep away from that clearing. At daybreak on the second day I found myself near the work site with my hounds. Danny's new men had already sawed the spar for stove wood. There were fresh jets of sawdust in the dirt where they'd cut it to length. Danny was rummaging the carcass of the yarder when he saw me. "Hey, Billy," he shouted, "some sonofabitch took out my spar and my yarder." He had the brow of an angel when he said it, and it was a wonder to me that a man like Danny could carry himself so pure and so wronged. But just that quick, I saw myself—not so different from him as I had been.

My hounds were crooning, a sign the trail had suddenly gone live, and I knew they'd be high notes over the ridge in a matter of minutes, so I waved at Danny like the man of leisure I'd suddenly become, thanks to him. I put my eyes to the ground for track. I admit it did my heart good to see I'd given him pause, made him take stock of a shift in his stature in the universe. Maybe what I'd done was the start of a true downward spiral for Danny's life. All I know is, he really did go bankrupt after that.

ONE DAY five years later I was driving to Discovery Bay to shoe a horse for Joe Cooper, when I saw a man walking at the side of the road. It was pouring rain and he was thumbing without looking as he walked.

I pulled over, thinking it could be me anytime now, since I was odd-jobbing it to hold things together these days, one step ahead of the devil. The guy opened the truck door, tossed his lunch bucket onto the seat, and climbed in. When he turned his head, I saw it was Danny. He'd aged considerably, to the point it made me wonder if I looked as bad. There'd been a twinkle in his eyes in our logging days, and he'd had charm that could cause a man to put aside his better judgment.

"Billy!" he said, like I was someone he'd been missing,

and he put out his hand. We caught hold of each other's palms and gave a squeeze. Rain was pelting the windshield. I could smell his clothes, wet and acrid in a mix of wood smoke and denim.

I was driving the same amazing piece of junk as when I'd worked for him, and we remarked on the sturdy nature of junk, that it should be given more credit on the world's balance sheet. "I'm not much better than a piece of junk myself," Danny said, and smiled. I was glad to hear something in his voice that meant this wasn't such a calamity for him to admit. At the same time, I saw that whatever he'd been traveling on earlier had left him. He could no longer strike deals, borrow money at banks, or convince a crew their paychecks were just around the corner.

"I'm splitting shakes in Chimacum," he told me. I looked down at one of his hands, resting palm-up near the lunch bucket, and I saw it was torn all to hell. We didn't talk for a stretch while I chanced it around a string of trailer houses leaving the west-end campgrounds in the downpour.

"I got me an indoor toilet again," I volunteered, as if to let him know I'd improved on where I'd been in our final days, when he'd joked that he'd advance me one crescent moon for my outhouse door.

What does one piece of junk say to another piece of junk anyway, going down the road? We talked a little more damage. One of his kids had turned wild as rhubarb in August, he said, and his wife's ex-husband had recently flipped his lid, rushed into their house one morning, yanked the phone off the wall, then lunged out again, using it as a walkie-talkie to God.

"I wish I had connections like that," Danny said, and

laughed in something akin to his old self. I told him how my drunken renter had run over and killed my favorite hound. I even exaggerated the state of my finances, telling him I was down to washing cars at the Jack-Pot, trying to steal customers from the cheerleaders on Sundays.

It was still raining when I came to my turnoff. I pulled over to let him out. He stepped onto the roadside, then reached back into the cab and offered me his beaten-up hand again. I leaned across the seat and took it, then let it go. I looked down and waited as he slammed the truck door. For a few moments I idled in the truck and watched him start off down the road without looking back.

The amazing thing was that there was still a lot left to Danny, even with his life savvy and charm out of the way. It occurred to me that if revenge is sweet, it's because it is also more than a little sad, sad and a weight to carry. And more often than not, we mistake sadness for sweetness.

When I glanced in my side-view, Danny was swinging his black lunch bucket and holding out his thumb. Cars were passing him up, one after the other. I considered turning around and driving him to Chimacum myself, just to save having to think of him cast out that way, a man without so much as a piece of junk to drive down the road.

But the past is a sure bullet with no mission but forward. I could feel it zinging straight through the stray, half-smart thoughts I wanted to have about my life or the fate of Danny Gunnerson. So I just kept herding my piece of junk down the road, to shoe a horse for Joe Cooper, a horse not unlike Joe, with more than a few bad rumors attached to it. Joe's ten-year-old granddaughter had named the horse Renegade, a name that gave me pause, thinking how even a kid knows, without being told, that wildness ought to be honored, ought to be called to. Like a horse named Renegade, that I was about to humiliate by pounding nails into its hooves to hold on rims of steel.

Chilean hummers were once dubbed "resurrected" birds because they were speedily aroused from torpid states by being warmed within the bosoms of women.

Venison

Pie

from the Journal of a Contemporary Hybrid

This peninsula, which is nearly an island, has mountains with names anyone would be proud to give as an address. To the southwest is Round Mountain and next to that Blue Mountain, with a road winding to its top called Blue Mountain Road.

Saying "Blue Mountain Road" is such a pleasure that I often route my guests over the top of Blue Mountain, then up the eastern side of this neighboring mountain where, some ten years ago, I built my cabin. True, it's a long way around, but it's still the best way. Nearby are Elk Mountain and Deer Mountain, named for animals here aplenty at one time, creatures many now consider pests if they show themselves when their water or food becomes scarce.

My favorite is Lost Mountain, a little to the east. I spent a lot of time as a child on the flank of this mountain with my parents, who were stump farmers, so I suppose it will always be my favorite—though naturally I am also partial to where I live, Dog Mountain. No one called the mountain this until recently. Even now it's a name I only tolerate, the way the ruby-throated hummingbird, or rufous-breasted hermit, or Anna's hummingbird might tolerate being called such, if they could hover long enough to be schooled in the trespass of any name. This mountain's original designation, Hummingbird Mountain, derived from a legend about a woman who'd left an early settlement in the region to live on her own.

There were suppositions about how this woman came to be accompanied by a halo of hummingbirds, which appeared to be feasting on the invisible energy that radiated from her. Wherever she went on the mountain, foraging for berries and mushrooms, hummingbirds moved with her.

An initial story began to accumulate about this woman in the time white men were writing in their journals, just as I—a woman with the hybrid pedigree of a hobo stew—am writing now in mine. These early journal writers put down all the details, peculiarities, and misconceptions regarding Indians in this then wild Washington Territory. A Lieutenant John Meares was scribbling about a chief named Callicum who slept, he wrote, "with his head on a bag of human skulls every night."

It was a popular misconception in those days that practices unthinkable to white men, such as cannibalism, were enjoyed with great relish by Indians. Such crude beliefs perhaps were deemed necessary in the ongoing scheme of appropriation. This propensity for gruesome fabrications allowed a great chasm of mistrust and incredulity, creating a veritable gorge of mistaken identity between Indians and whites, ongoing to this writing.

The woman of Hummingbird Mountain had witnessed the occasion of a venison pie presented by Captain Vancouver in 1792 to the Nootka Indians at Admiralty Inlet. I heard this story of venison pie when I was very young. It had been handed down to others by the woman who witnessed it. Later I was able to confirm the story when I read James Swan's account. Swan, like most journal writers, would likely understand my love of how life overlaps its own footprints with question marks at times, as when a legend overwhelms history, or history, in statuesque sentences, waterfalls past anyone's individual accounting, sweeping aside in a vast current the singular intention that was the lightning rod to a moment. Yet Swan is placid where I would be exclamatory. Imagine, for instance, Vancouver's surprise as the leader of the Nootkas flung the venison pie over Vancouver's very head into the icy waters of the inlet. What might be written then of this episode in the great language of equilibrium?

There was a lot of consternation by Vancouver and his men over what they considered the pure ignorance and wastefulness of the Indians on that occasion, for venison pie was a dish said to have been invented by French traders with the presumably wild, yet indigenous palates of Indians in mind. As Vancouver watched the venison pie float out toward the Pacific, feasted upon by seagulls, he must have puzzled greatly as to what had gone awry.

Yes, that would do, very nicely. But we know something more when we imagine a woman standing on the shore. The woman witnesses the floating pie in the current from a short distance. She moves closer to the two groups of men and sees that finally, after turning their backs and showing signs of the greatest disgust, the leader of the tribe, whose name is unrecorded, begins to make plain to Vancouver that he and his men do not eat human flesh. He is eloquent, and he does not use *few words,* as accounts have misrecorded. The gist of his response is that the white men can keep their stinking cuisine to themselves. Further, he allows they may feed such pies to their dogs. The leader then turns his back and walks an important distance away.

Only when one of Vancouver's men went back to the ship and hauled the haunch of a deer to the banquet site, in order to certify the origin of the venison pie, were the Indians at last persuaded to sit "at table" over still more venison pies and to sup peaceably with their white hosts. Later speculation regarding the initial refusal of the pie centered on the fact that it had been seasoned heavily with pepper, of which "the Indians could not bear the least particle," according to Swan.

The story of venison pie is one I like to tell when anyone is arrogant enough to think they can go through life without misunderstanding, when in fact, at times they are downright reinventing the people around them. "Let me tell you a story about venison pie," I say to them. And, in fact, we all need reinventing from time to time in order to delineate the boundaries of our recalcitrance, which is also an underestimated form of vigor.

But I had begun to tell the legend of this witness-woman. Instead, I veered away, like a hummingbird sparring with a crow, to speak of venison pie and erroneous cannibals. But veering is courtship and, like the hummingbird with its metallic, iridescent sheen ruffling its breastbone, I face into the sun to best show plumage when I dive into story. I lose sight of time and the world and everything in it. Perhaps this straying is, itself, a form of female ecstasy I initiate as I write.

Certainly there are occasions when I wish I had a peppery venison pie of my own to throw at certain cannibals-of-the-real who daily infect the sacredness of the journey, whatever our origins. It has been repugnant to me, for instance, to have anyone tell me I don't "look Indian," even when, with the utmost care, they couch it with: "But you don't *look* Native American."

It's true that my unknown amount of Cherokee, added to my one sixteenth extinct and uncertifiable Kar-wee'wee, plus my pinch of Ojibwa, joined to or departing from Finnish blood, further mixed or assaulted by Pennsylvania Dutch, doesn't show up as much as one in my circumstances, a bearer of legends, could wish. My bloodline can and must be thrown into question. But no one is arguing about the Finns in my past. I say my ancestry must be questioned because this questioning, this veering of others toward and away, is also a kind of aggressive, but necessary, courtship.

Nonetheless, I am certain, even though it is now unverifiable, that I am related, at the very least through spirit and desire, to the Kar-wee'wee woman I am speaking about here. One must have patience with obscured origins. I forgo the great pleasure of hurling a venison pie at those who wish to deny my attempts to connect or to reconnect, to gather up the shards and bits of my amalgamated unbelonging. I walk away. I turn my back when they want to see my credentials. I become the cannibal of my authenticity, which is the authenticity of river, of mountain. It runs. It stands.

BUT MANY things can be known from the diligent study of others. Female hummingbirds of a few species, for instance, such as the Annas, are able to manage more than one nest at a time, even though the male is of little help in the actual rearing of the young. The language of this knowledge is passionate in the exactness of its observations and attracts me like the nectar of azaleas:

> *As the nestlings become fledglings and head into flight from one downy sleeve laced with spider web, the female will be feeding a brood in another nest, and perhaps warming eggs in yet another. Each of these broods will have been fathered by a different mate. Since hummingbirds aren't particular about mating with different species, the great variety of hybrids is impressive.*

I am fascinated, it's true, by any profusion of hybrids, as was the woman of Hummingbird Mountain. She felt a kinship, according to legend, with these female hummingbirds who chose not to trust the supposed security of the nest. Rather they preferred the backup nest, and the backup nest to that. They also enjoyed the variety of mates they could expect each spring. They didn't waste energy worrying about any mate's fidelity, since it was expected that each male would also have been busy with at least one other female. As she admired her male consorts, she did not know that the beauty of their plumage depended as much on *refraction* and *interference* as upon pigment. She had not read the books, the journals of those who would later study hummingbirds, where it is observed that *radiance derives from the position of the feather.* She experienced only their unique fiery glow and the "something more" that the ever-stunted language of beauty can only gesture toward.

She became the protector and benefactor of all inhabitants on Hummingbird Mountain, but especially of female hummingbirds. When the local Indians heard of her, they said she had likely once been a hummingbird herself and had recently become their human slave or shadow-spirit as a result of having disgraced them in some way—as happens, for instance, when a hummingbird has sipped from forbidden flowers or taken too many mates or abandoned nests before chicks are hatched—a great invisible realm of possible wrongdoing.

Nonetheless, in her human state, she went happily about her task of being productively frenzied about everything, including the job of expelling an overabundance of arrogant male hummingbirds which came to steal nectar within the *luk,* or mating area. She could approximate the swift diving and whirring sounds of hummingbirds at a distance of eighty yards, unsettling the air like a deck of cards being shuffled. She managed this by some trick of pursing her mouth and bringing air all the way from her toes into her nasal passages, then expelling it through her nostrils with a great outward rush. As she gradually took on her new identity of Hummingbird-Bride, she made a second paradise of the open meadows and brambled riversides, clearing saplings away to let sunlight better illuminate the wildflowers— fireweed, foxglove, red currant. But she also offered the refractory powers of her spirit.

At some point, according to her legend, she passed with ease and honor into the form of a female hummingbird. There is some doubt from those who carried this story forward as to whether, in hummingbird form, she was ever quite as happy as she'd been as Hummingbird-Bride. Perhaps hers was one of those punishments which has no exit, and which simply has to be tolerated and lived through in its endless succession of forms.

I ALSO HAVE been trying to make the best of circumstances here on Hummingbird Mountain since it became Dog Mountain. Those who have heard my oft-recounted stories of this place can see that such a name carries not the least hint of its rich past, nor of its benefactor and protecting presence, the woman who became a hummingbird. "Dog Mountain" is a blatant slur on the steady industry and magical character of such a mountain.

Under the name Hummingbird Mountain there was the belief that the entire mountain could actually hover above earth while it stretched into the clouds, past broad wings of rain, to collect a sweetness it then gave back as still more nourishing rain. When fog rolled in from Fuca Strait (the old territorial name of these waters) and swirled the base of the mountain, it was even easier for literal-minded visitors to observe that the mountain did, indeed, hover above earth. But verification of the miraculous forbids altitude: *the mountain hovered.*

Why it should fall to me to defend this mountain's former identity, I don't know. Probably it has to do with my life on the mountain, simply being here and being able to write in my journal. For, as they say in love, proximity is more than half the battle. Still, it's true I am unqualified in a way perhaps not dissimilar to Hummingbird-Bride, who was unsuited to be the bride of any human form.

I have dared to carry some small shards of my self-assumed relation to Hummingbird-Bride, but was unable, in any case, to save this mountain from its disparagement as Dog Mountain. It is suspected that there are rich deposits of ore inside this mountain, a tempting enough prospect for it to be sold to mining interests so the proceeds can be used to build not one, but two, gambling casinos. (Already the muffled click of dice across the felt-covered table pulls at local brain stems.)

As the dog of Dog Mountain, I realize a certain perverse stature. There is significance and a certain rightness in my having been called "dog," for just as dogs were precursors to the horse as carriers of burdens, so am I unaccountably the transport of this mountain's legends.

There exists among many peoples a great respect for the spirits of "place." Accordingly, I celebrate fierce spirits in the long beaks of the hummingbirds which nest everywhere on this mountain. Can it be that because I'm here to tell its legend, the mountain recalls its hovering, as well as its entrance into its present torpor? Why am I so haunted by the velocity of multiple hummingbird hearts pumping twelve hundred beats a minute? I am sure of one thing: that this mountain would vanish before it would allow itself to be sold for a throw of dice or the snap of an ace on a gaming table.

It is obvious that I have set my own flower-honed beak among the sword ferns. The spirit of my courtly veering is devotion. When I pass, the sight-blasted eye of crow stares down. I have been known to stand heedless in a certain waterfall that remembers a woman who became a hummingbird. I offer myself pensively, letting the water pour over and away from me, as I consider this mountain's rushing, its democratic gathering up, to which I am a kind of lumpish, undifferentiated, fleshy offering.

For those who wish to come here, I advise a route by way of Lost Mountain. There is, however, the warning that those who set out do not always arrive. Whether this is the residue of some irresolvable punishment or an adventurous advantage, I cannot say. Only that sometimes traders conveying overspiced venison pies, or the vision of a woman in a meadow haloed by humming-birds, or the pitchy curiosity of legend disguised as history, fruitfully impedes the sojourner. This is the hazard, the bright and barbarous invitation of Dog Mountain.

In Wisconsin during the 1840s, a tavern keeper advertised:

> *There will be* RARE SPORT *at which time a* HE
> BEAR *will be baited by relays of five dogs every
> thirty minutes, and that a she bear will be barbe-
> cued for dinner.*

*Bearbaiting was so popular among the forty-niners that
over a hundred men made a good living scouring the
mountains, trapping bears by various methods. To provide animals for these gruesome shows became almost a
regular profession.*

Peninsula Daily News, August 9, 1996:

*A Ukrainian immigrant convicted of using snares to ille-
gally kill bears and then selling their parts on the black
market has been sentenced to three months in jail in
Spokane . . . a former professional hunter from the
Ukraine, [he] was convicted of selling the paws, claws
and gallbladders from at least four bears that agents say
he caught in the snares.*

To

Dream

of

Bears

If you could get Tivari to talk about his fear of water, he'd say it had to do with his Romanian mother's vivid descriptions of a drowning she'd witnessed on the last day of a summer holiday at the Black Sea. Mostly, though, he wouldn't talk about his phobia, as if some dangerous, yet-to-be-crossed body of water might overhear and take note of him.

"I flew over an ocean to get here. Now I'm sleeping on water and taking a boat to work," Tivari said to me one day in disbelief. We were housed on a float camp snugged offshore in a small bay near our logging site on Prince of Wales Island.

My friendship with Tivari had begun in Washington State in 1965, during a logging job near Sappho. We'd both been in our early twenties, cutting the '21 Blow on a six-month job, so there'd been plenty of time to get to know each other. The "Big Blow," as the windstorm was called, had leveled an entire forest in 1921 at the ocean end of the Olympic Peninsula. Cutting in those return stands was an eerie undertaking and if the wind came up, we respected it and called it a day.

Tivari had long, sinewy arms like a wrestler. He wore his black beard well trimmed and this made his milk-white teeth seem false. While the rest of us were calling our tatters fashionable, Tivari's overalls would be mended, because he was good with a needle—something taught him by his Romanian mother. If anyone had a splinter in his palm or needed a wound lanced, he would call for Tivari as if he were a doctor.

We always knew he was at hand because he carried a transistor radio and tape deck everywhere. He loved opera or any serious classical station. When reception was poor, as it mostly was, he would punch in a tape. He often turned up the volume until we had to shout to be heard, and there were times even I missed the silence of the trees. No question, we were the only gyppos in the world cutting timber to *Aida*. The men joked freely about Tivari's music, and I once heard him called the Volga Boatman, though not to his face.

"You think trees don't have souls? What are you, some dumb stumps?" he shouted, until the word "stumps" echoed in the clear island air. He contended that the forest was in the presence of its tragedy and its beauty when he played this music. "If I had to fall," he announced, "let me hear 'Twilight of the Gods' while I'm crashing down." Tivari also applied music as a preventative against drowning and would sing along to the best of his ability as we motored across the bay between our float camp and work site.

By the time I hit Alaska, I had a healthy respect for what it took to keep any logger's fears in harness. We were at the prime of our lives, our pleasures on hold back in the towns we'd left. Tivari's music came to represent more than what we were missing. It stood for gentility and ease we'd probably never get. I found myself enjoying the rigorous emotional keening of those operatic voices—and I'm sure there were one or two others who more than submitted to its mournful intoxication. I even took to carrying a spare set of batteries in case Tivari's should run down, as they often did. Tivari cutting a tree in silence—now that was an experience to be avoided, the way others avoided Saturday night whores.

Tivari did not avoid the ladies. It was as if, having escaped a week of water crossings, he had an impulse to reward himself, to drown in the calculated attentions of women. He paid over his earnings and this brought all he could drink, plus a sodden sort of company into Sunday.

When all was said, Tivari transcended his breakout time. I'd seen him so wasted he couldn't get his chain around his saw blade, but by the next workday he was still the best bushler and blowdown bucker there was. He knew that a blowdown can look dead, but have vicious turns of life left in it that could whip around and run a man through with his own saw. He also knew the cardinal rule of such cutting—when to quit.

Tivari, in short, was, by nature and necessity, an artist of the moment. To work, eat, and move daily in his company was to feel that any instant might break open to hilarity or sorrow or some joyful clamor that lifted, for an instant, the weight of the day, and could be traded out as story during the relentless daylight evenings of Alaskan summers.

"Tivari," someone would say, "tell us about the time you wrestled the bear." And it was true, or should have been if it wasn't, that Tivari had once wrestled a bear in a logging camp near Homer. He took his shirt off on occasion to display a scar that ran diagonally across his back to his right hip. The bear, he said, had been raised in captivity by a young boy, then sold by his parents for spectacle.

The match he'd fought was not the first for the bear. Word reached camp that it had badly mauled the last man it had similarly encountered, so expectations were tilted heavily in favor of the bear. Tivari realized from the start that the animal intended to do damage. It entered the makeshift ring with its head low and its ears back. A raking moan unwound from the bear. This woeful sound was punctuated with chuffing noises. Tivari's mates were there to cheer him on, though several of them, he later learned, had placed money on the bear.

"I held his jaws like this," he said, grabbing the head of the logger sitting next to him and forcing his mouth wide, "and I gave that bear mouth-to-mouth resuscitation." He did not demonstrate this last. "I might as well have poured gasoline down that bear and dropped in a lit match," Tivari said, playing to his audience. He claimed that prior to the fight he'd eaten a powerful amount of garlic, and that while he was breathing the bear into submission, it had raked its claw down his back.

On one occasion I saw a logger who kept hounds attempt to get Tivari to discuss bear hunting. It ended with the man slapping down a hunting magazine and telling him to "read up" if he wanted to pretend he knew anything about bears. Then the man pulled the ultimate dismissive and called him "a goddamned environmentalist." But Tivari was beyond the assumed slur of "environmental." He had set his own course for understanding and valuing bears. He held no false pieties about the animal he clearly loved and, before anything, he was a storyteller.

Each time Tivari removed his shirt, the scar ran before us like an angry river in which he'd narrowly missed drowning. We were believers then, carried beyond faith, into the place where story outleaps what happened and still, in some cow-over-the-moon fashion, stays true. A creature or someone had raked a knife, a scythe, or a claw deeply down Tivari's back, and it became the hieroglyphic of his past survivals, of which we were unlikely ever to hear details.

In 1972, when he was thirty, Tivari had, against his mother's pleas, gone back to Romania in search of his father. His father had become a political prisoner in 1969, under Ceauşescu's regime, and had not been heard from since. Not surprisingly Tivari managed, in short order, to get himself thrown into prison. We'd heard his descriptions of cold beyond cold, how the men would lend each other warmth in the clammy, rat-infested recesses of the Bucharest prison. But whatever Tivari had experienced there made him fog over with silence when anyone came too near the site of those experiences.

"No, friend, don't ask," he'd say. "I lost some brothers there, and that's not the worst of it."

Whatever the worst was, we would only catch glimpses in his desperate drinking bouts. I assumed it had something to do with whatever he'd discovered about the fate of his father. But someone started a rumor that Tivari had been castrated in prison and that this was why he was forever begging the whores to "take pity" on him—an unfortunate phrase he would utter during pangs of drunken abandonment on the floating tug *The Gallant Lady*, aboard which few of the ladies were exactly gallant, though, by report, they had other favorable attributes.

"Take pity!" Tivari would implore from inside the cramped belowdecks compartments of the tug. His voice drifted to those of us at float camp who had girlfriends or wives to whom we were safely sworn. The word "pity" never had such resonance for me as when I heard it, from my bunk, in Tivari's unmistakable voice, torn across the short Alaska night, like the plea of a man with his head on a chopping block. I did have occasion, in the casual life of men thrown together in close quarters, to be able to report at large that Tivari had his equipment intact. Still, I suspected something completely unmanned him when it came to women.

Nonetheless, the more fickle the woman, the more ardently Tivari would pursue. We all felt he'd topped his mark when he fastened on a woman we called the Blond Bomber. Her true name was Rena and she was married to our hook tender, Al Worthington. Al had situated Rena on shore in a cabin an hour from camp. We were under pressure to get the timber down, and had light enough to cut until 3 A.M., if we wanted to take it. Because the pace was just short of killing, Al visited Rena at weekly intervals and spent most nights at float camp.

The Bomber, on occasion, and much to Al's dismay, made appearances at camp. She was a showy woman with Marilyn Monroe–style bleached-blond hair. Her breasts were a prominent feature and she dressed to their advantage, her waist cinched so tightly that her voice seemed to come from her nostrils. On one of her sudden visits to camp, Rena caught Tivari's eye. Not long after, I noticed he would be away nights when Al stayed at camp.

Rena had a passion for clothes that bordered on mania. She kept Al working seven days a week to buy her the latest styles, which she ordered from catalogs and had delivered by float plane to the cove near her cabin.

Once Tivari made up his mind to have Rena, his campaign was swift and determined. He took her to Anchorage, behind Al's back, and fitted her out like a runway model. Then he paraded her through the bars, snatching the envy of men and the jaundiced scrutiny of the barflies. It was a heady concoction that fueled them into their elopement out of Alaska.

WHEN I next heard of Tivari, he'd moved Rena to Aberdeen, where once again he found himself living at the edge of water. I had recently come down from Alaska when he phoned to ask me to partner up with him. It would save me time and money, he said, if I stayed with him and Rena.

In Aberdeen I had a close look at how Tivari was managing life. I was glad Rena hadn't shut down his love of opera. The tide lapped not a hundred yards from the door and he kept the windows open so the music swirled out to fishing and pleasure boats offshore. A revival CD, *Caruso in Song*, was on before we left in the morning, accompanied us to work, and played into the night when we returned. It amounted to total immersion. His favorite cut, "Guardanno 'a Luna," lapped away consciousness that it was even playing.

My friend so indulged Rena in her quest for the flashiest, most outrageous clothes that there didn't seem to be money left for much else. They had one comfortable piece of living room furniture, an antique maroon velvet couch, of which Tivari was inordinately proud.

"Think of it," he would say, when he'd entered his

nightly ritual of cauterizing the day with drink. "I've taken thousands of dollars' worth of clothes off that wicked woman right where you're sitting."

Rena would be propped in bed with one of her fashion catalogs. But Tivari seemed in no hurry to go to bed these nights. He wanted to regale me with stories of bears. How Indian hunters had used every part of the bear when they'd killed it—eaten the meat, made the teeth and claws into charms, given the paws to their medicine men, turned its skin into blankets and clothing, melted down the fat for cooking oil, even twisted its intestines into bowstrings.

"No one will ever use us so well, my friend," Tivari said, licking his beard from his white teeth and bowing his head toward his jelly glass with its potent triple shot of *ţuica*—a rheumy-looking plum brandy he'd learned to make in Romania. Tivari's philosophy was simply that one of the worst things that could happen to a creature, man or beast, was not to be used up, to be in some sense wasted.

Tivari continued to lean over the knees of his perfectly patched overalls, telling me how the Pueblos had, according to accounts, believed their medicine men could actually change themselves into bears. He'd discovered the library and read deeply on the subject. He'd become curious about a passage in one of the books which described how the Michigan tribes, the Cree and the Ojibwas, were said to have turned against black bears and killed them for government bounties after smallpox had devastated their tribes. "The Bear Wars," Tivari called them. "Some say the Indians believed those bears were in a conspiracy against them. That the bears could have healed them, but they refused, and let them die of smallpox. But remember, these are white historians. Nobody, except maybe the ghosts of those Indians, really knows why they started to kill bears for bounty."

I learned much later that Tivari's mother's maiden name was Ursu, which means "bear," and may have partly accounted for his fascination and respect for the animal. He could snap out figures about the early decimation of bears in America like sparks from a campfire: West Virginia hunters who took 8,000 black bears for skins early in the 1800s; trappers in the Dakotas who racked up 746 skins in five years through 1805.

"Sportsmen will be quick as a bullet to tell you today this country is overrun with bears, and in some places maybe it's true, so they're never entirely wrong. But somebody sure took care of those black bears in the Dakotas. No bear problem there now," Tivari said and fell silent. We could hear the waves rushing against the logs below the house. They tossed and hissed, then sighed into the huge dark that was the Pacific. Finally Tivari began to tell about the execution of eight bears in Yosemite National Park in 1979—"problem bears" who'd had a history of bad interactions with humans and paid the ultimate price.

"They kept files on them, and when they had enough evidence, they shot those bears," Tivari said, as if the bears were the brothers he'd lost in the prisons of Bucharest. At some point I asked him how the Indians had been able to kill bears at all, if, as he said, they had considered them healers.

"Those bears, even when they were dead, just somehow went back to live in the forests. You couldn't really kill them. That's what the Indians believed. I'm not going to die either," he said with a grin. "I'm just going back to the forest." Then he roused himself and found a pillow for me so I could make my bed on the velvet couch. I watched him careen toward the bedroom, where I imagined Rena lay asleep, wrapped in the sexiest negligee money could buy.

That night I fell into dreams of bears. I was hopelessly attempting to frighten off one with a water pistol. I pulled the trigger to no avail, then managed to shoot a pitiful stream of water toward its toothy snout as it advanced, upright like a man. The steady sound of collapsing and retreating waves against the logs on the beach came through the open window to mix with menace in the dream, and I was glad for daylight and the smell of coffee.

"That's good, to dream of bears," Tivari said, the next morning as we filled our coffee bottles. "It means they've noticed you. They're looking out for you. But I'd drop the water pistol if I were you."

Someone besides bears had noticed me. Rena, from the blue caves of her sleepy morning glances, seemed to have fastened inordinately on my needs. She rustled between us in a red silk kimono embroidered with dragons, marshaling us in the dawn light for the arrival of the "crummy" to take us to work. I had a sinking feeling that Tivari would soon have his hands full. The prospect was wide and cheerless as sunrise over a clear-cut. Even though I'd done nothing to invite Rena's attentions that morning, and even though they'd passed seemingly without my friend's noticing, they left me with a guilty residue, as if her assumptions about the fragile nature of friendship had caused me to call myself into question. It was luck and providence that our work suddenly ran out and I moved to another part of the state.

AN INTERVAL of months passed with no logging to be found. Then I took work as a "casualty," longshoring. It was good pay with overtime. The next thing I knew I was traveling to unload a ship in Aberdeen. I was glad to have an excuse to visit Tivari. I'd gotten married by this time and rented a small house in Port Orchard. My wife worked as a nurse in a retirement home. She wore a uniform and was as far from the Blond Bomber as they come. Word along the gossip line was that Tivari and Rena were openly at odds. She'd taken a job as a cocktail waitress at a local resort and had subsequently overstimulated the imaginations of some of her customers.

"There are bears who get to be panhandlers," Tivari said to me on my first night back, with Rena out of earshot. "People feed them—panhandlers are mostly females—and it's like signing their death warrants." We were talking about bears and we weren't. Tivari had bought a freezerful of beef which sat on the back porch, and all week we ate steaks and prime rib, cooked to a bloodless turn by Rena.

When I arrived back at Tivari's after a three-day weekend with my wife, havoc had struck. A window had been shattered on the back porch. I looked in at the freezer, and saw the kitchen door standing open onto the porch. I walked around and glanced through the front window. The space once occupied by the velvet couch was bare.

It was scorching, hitting the mid-nineties. My mind fastened on locating a dark bar and a cold beer. As I drew up in front of the Red Ranch Tavern, I spotted Tivari's pickup. White packages of partly frozen beef were heaped on the velvet couch in the truck bed. Blood was soaking into the couch in the noonday heat.

Inside the tavern I found Tivari. He recognized me through the beery dark as I approached, raised his right hand, extended his index finger and drew it swiftly across his throat in a cutting motion. He made a gurgling noise like the sound of waves withdrawing over small stones, then turned back to his drink. I took the stool beside him. The music was country and western and I knew he must be punishing himself. Or maybe the stock dilemmas of opera and country music had run together for him of late. I didn't know what to say. My life, by comparison, seemed far from the turnstile future he was meeting with Rena.

"A guy actually came up to me today and asked did I know where he could get himself a bear's gallbladder," Tivari said in disgust, offering me a door into his general despair. It seems the Chinese had been paying big money for bear gallbladders. They believed them to be aphrodisiacs. Tivari allowed that any number of bears all over the country had been killed recently for their gallbladders alone.

"Bastard," Tivari said. "Sonofabitch," he added for good measure. "And no part of him worth killing for."

I rested my arm across my friend's back. I knew that just under my forearm ran the long angry scar that Tivari claimed a bear had given him. Whether or not it had actually been a bear, I felt he'd earned its connection by now, through respect and his earnest attempt to discover something of their nature and history. Male black bears, he'd been quick to tell me, lived and died mostly alone.

But today he had another story in mind. Soon the Black Sea stretched before us in the early dawn. The lifeguards had not yet come on duty. His Romanian mother was still a young woman, collecting seashells on the last day of her summer holiday. Since my own mother had died when I was a baby, I had no such stories or memories. Consequently, Tivari's recounting of this incident concerning his mother held a fascination for me.

"Suddenly a man's voice crying for help caused my

mother to look up," Tivari said. "She saw a man on shore leap into the waves and swim to a man who was surely drowning. She watched the swimmer catch the man by his hair and begin to pull him toward land. She was taking this in with her eyes, but also her soul, she told me. Somehow, after a long time in the water, the swimmer lost his grip on the man. When he reached shore, he stepped out of the water alone.

"A woman ran up to my mother," Tivari said. "She asked, 'Did he drown? Did a man drown?' 'Yes,' my mother told her, 'I'm sorry, he's lost. He couldn't be saved.' Then the woman said, 'That was *my* man,' and began to wail. She rushed toward the sea and into the waves. She stood up to her knees in the water and cried, 'Give him back! Have mercy! Give him back!' But the sea just kept being the sea.

"My mother cast her eyes back and forth," Tivari said, "but she saw only waves, rising and falling. Then a young girl came toward the woman in the waves. She was weeping and she held out a man's shirt. That must be the drowned man's daughter, my mother thought. She watched the woman and daughter holding each other with the shirt between them. Then my mother took the shells she'd gathered, drew her arm back, and flung them hard into the sea.

"After that," Tivari said, "my mother was angry about bodies of water. When I was little she wouldn't let me swim with my friends. She'd tell me this story and warn me, until the only safe water for me was in a tap or on a postcard."

Unlike Tivari, I'd had no such warnings. No mother's fears to temper what I dared to do. My father had raised me to feel able for anything. "He can swim like a seal," my father had bragged. Tivari could not swim, but he admired those who could, as if they were specially gifted, like the opera singers he loved. He told me once about three troublesome Newfoundland bears whose swimming had brought them notoriety. They'd been removed from the mainland by park officials to an island in Bonavista Bay. But the next day the bears swam off the island through stormy waters, then they walked eleven miles back to their home territory. Tivari believed so much was coded into us, we'd probably never know why we did what we did.

"Mother Nature leaves a survival map in each of us," he said. "We just have to know how to read it. My mother read it, and it said: 'Keep your kid terrified of water.' But, my friend, you can drown anywhere."

Suddenly I remembered the blood-sodden couch and decided to try to move my friend.

"Tivari," I said. "I know a butcher with a big heart and an enormous freezer." He followed me unsteadily into the searing daylight. I opened the passenger side of the pickup and he obediently handed me the keys, then climbed in.

We drove to my friend's shop and stacked the beef in the corner of his walk-in freezer. Tivari took delight in the cold as we moved back and forth, dodging the hanging sides of beef and pork.

"Shut the door and take me out in the spring," he joked with typical bravado. Then he stepped from the freezer, grabbed the palm of my hand and pressed it to his chest. "Imagine, if I was a bear in hibernation, this heart would be down to eight beats a minute. We're nothing but halfway primitive meat compared to bears," he said and let my hand drop from his cold grasp.

Later that night I drove Tivari to another friend's to sober up and to sleep. This friend was a retired high school coach who'd recently gone through a divorce. We slept on mattresses on the floor of his workout room, among weights and fitness machines. The next morning we each showered and sampled my friend's wide spectrum of toiletries, then, smelling like pimps, drove to Tivari's house. As we parked at the back, I was somehow not surprised to see the sheriff coming off the porch to meet us. He had the clouded look of a man who's learned to expect the worst and is not often disappointed.

"Your wife says you stole her clothes. That right, Tivari?" the sheriff asked, retreating a few steps when he caught wind of us. Tivari didn't answer. "Your wife's down signing a restraining order on you," the sheriff said, and folded his arms in a gesture of contained official pleasure. "You want to tell me about the clothes?"

The sheriff and I followed my friend onto the porch. Tivari lifted the lid of the twenty-one-foot chest freezer and stepped back. Inside, frozen in a solid four-foot-deep block of ice, were the fur coats, sequined gowns, and sheer negligees of Rena's long career. We stared at the frozen garments, as if the Black Sea of his mother's story had suddenly risen up and deposited the congealed debris of a life. Tivari quietly bent over and pulled the electric plug.

We left the sheriff to inventory the damage and walked back toward the truck. Dried maps of blood splotched the cushions and arms of Tivari's velvet couch on the pickup bed. It looked like the site of a massacre. But I knew Tivari, as he took note of it, was probably recalling his misbegotten hopes with Rena, their late-night erotic rituals—reduced to this sad, unseemly display.

Tivari climbed behind the wheel and we drove to my truck at the tavern. We went inside for what I knew would become for him another drinking bout. I could stay with Tivari, but couldn't attempt to keep up with his drinking. I knew he was about to head over the top and out to sea. Soon images of his mother in a summer dress would surface like a strange obliterating sun.

These glimpses of her belonged so familiarly to me by now, they were nearly my own. I thought she had somehow made sure, across time and death, that I was there, next to her son. Her defiant gesture, as she'd thrown the shells back into the sea, seemed the long arc of her connection to me—a man drawn taut as a bowstring by things he did not understand and could not control. I was sure Tivari had no notion why he'd been held in lockstep with a woman like Rena, whose surface was glassy as a waveless sea. Likewise, I couldn't figure why I wasn't in my car driving hell-bent-for-leather for Port Orchard and my wife.

The jukebox had begun to play something so melancholy and awash with heartbreak that Tivari's voice from our Alaskan days rang out again across water and darkness—"Take pity!" And I did. I clung to his slumping form in the downward spiral of that music, swimming against fate and memory, with Tivari's thin hair wrapped around my fingers.

The audible tone created by the hummingbird's wings is actually an overtone, not the fundamental tone, which is too low to be heard . . .

The

Leper

When a place is too beautiful, there are repercussions. Such places attract disruptions, encroachments, noxious pollutants of sound and deed. Things of the daily sort that would pass unnoticed in an ugly suburb, or even on some normal residential street, work a vengeance here. It is a burden, I'm saying, to live where I live.

Below the house the bay is bright with water and light, and there is the wistful cry of gulls. But even now this is spoiled by the pounding of hammers against wood. My neighbor's porch steps are being rebuilt. The pounding should stay attached to this. But in this place of relative tranquillity my mind flings itself into gruesome possibilities: one moment there is the idea that a guillotine is being constructed; the next that a man-sized cross is being readied; or that someone is assembling a coffin, board by board, outside my window. But all the while it is only the domestic carpentry of my neighbor's workmen.

Nonetheless, there is privacy to be had here like no other. I can settle myself nicely into a sun-warmed chair and put my feet up on the railing and dream. But just then someone might knock at the door—the same neighbor who is building his steps, for instance, insisting, as he did once, that black ants have made a nest under the property and are threatening to carry away the entire hillside.

But not all disruptions to the beauty are entirely unpleasant. Some fall into the range of what one might call "spectacle."

Our house overlooks other well-kept houses in this development, which is situated outside a small seaport. One morning not long ago we looked down and saw a naked woman bicycling toward the tennis courts. It was raining. Not heavily, but enough that those who would have been going for their morning walks had stayed inside. I put the binoculars on the woman and watched as she entered the fenced, forbidden tennis court of our neighbor. She pedaled round and round the court in wide, opulent circles.

"What does she think she's doing?" my husband said, drying his hands on his darkroom apron. He had already been at work printing the latest photographs he'd taken of the mountains of our area. "She's got to be nuts," he said and reached for the binoculars. "Give me a break!" he said, and shoved them into my hands. I lifted them to my eyes and saw the woman had a message smeared on her back: COWARDS! it said in what I thought was lipstick.

"She probably knows everybody just picked up their binoculars," I said, handing the glasses back to him.

"Not bad-looking," my husband said, pressing the lenses to his face. "But old Rosenthal won't like it a bit, her ruining the surface on his tennis court."

But no one came out of Rosenthal's house and no one interfered with the woman's methodical desecration of the tennis court. The rain kept falling. We ate our toast in the breakfast nook and went about our daily tasks. We had learned by now that it was best not to devote too much time to such occurrences.

Sometimes the assault on our tranquillity persists and becomes an unwelcome, permanent part of our days, as when one of our neighbors, against all regulations, erected a bell tower in which he installed a carillon. At precisely six o'clock in the evening, it played notes approximating "Amazing Grace." There were complaints, of course. A vote was taken, as for any adjustment in our community. But unaccountably, there were more consenting households than not, so the carillon became a fixture in our days beside the beautiful light-shattered bay.

But when all seems *too* calm from without, my husband and I become uneasy. It is then that a rupture is most likely to come from within. Thus, with a certain false confidence, we noted that during the past several days of hammering nothing untoward had happened—no arguments had broken out between us, no malfunctioning of appliances, no lost items that needed searching for. The snarl of saws, the thudding of hammer blows seemed to have absolved our days of a beauty too open to decay or of the wearied bliss of resort havens, which our area most resembles.

But today, just as we began to settle into the relative comfort of this routine, the phone rang. It was my friend Jerome, a sculptor. He is a man who treads an uneasy path between fear and despair, and someone who could ill afford to be calling me at two o'clock in the afternoon on a weekday, when telephone rates are at their peak.

"Jerome," I said, "this is costing an arm and a leg."

"I know. I can't help it," he said grimly. "I'm furious and I can't stop myself. Catlin was supposed to call me two hours ago. I'm about to be evicted. I've got to get payment on those pieces he sold. Why didn't he call when he said he would? Why does he torture me like this?"

Catlin is the gallery manager who handles Jerome's work. He is a conscientious fellow who had recently taken a lover and fallen into domestic problems.

"I'm sure there's a reasonable explanation," I said, trying to wipe flour off my hands. I'd begun to roll out pie dough when the phone rang. I cradled the receiver on my shoulder and continued to shape the oval of dough into a circle with the rolling pin as I listened. Jerome was always working himself into a frenzy over things normal people would have shrugged off. But he could take nothing for granted. There was no such thing as an unwilled act. If someone failed to answer his call or letter, it meant one thing and one thing only—malicious intentional neglect. He was forever bludgeoning himself with imagined betrayals, so much so that his anguished phone calls brought ridicule from our mutual friends, including one who even bragged that he kept crossword puzzles near the phone to amuse himself during calls from Jerome. My husband was similarly unsympathetic to my friend's panics and turmoils.

"Tell him everyone hates him. Who'd want to call him anyway?" my husband shouted, then slammed the door to his darkroom. As I say, we live in a beautiful place and this places an unnecessary strain on our lives.

"Jerome," I said, "something must have come up. Catlin's a fair man. He means only the best. Remember, he's just been through a hard time, and it still isn't easy. Maybe he isn't attending to business as well as he should."

"You can say that again!" Jerome said. "It's no excuse. I'm tired of their breakups, their influenzas and visiting in-laws. They won't get away with it!" I thought I heard him bang his fist on something. But just then there was an awful pounding close by that I mistakenly took for the sounds of the carpenters. I put my free hand over my ear and pressed the receiver against my head with the other. Jerome's plaintive voice continued to enter my ear despite the noise.

"Why? Why should I waste my forgiveness on such people?" he was saying.

"Jerome, dear, why don't you hang up and write me a letter. This is costing a fortune," I said. Yet the moment I suggested it, a fear rose up in me. Jerome had once tried to gas himself but had been discovered by his landlady. Another time he'd thrown himself in front of a passing car. Luckily the driver had slammed on the brakes in time. Jerome had actually been committed to an institution for the mentally disturbed for a brief period during our college days—a time during which he got hold of a packet of matches and inflicted burn wounds on fifteen percent of his body. He joked about these scars now as "outbreaks of insanity." I was worried by his silence, yet this too was a ritual of these conversations. As I listened for his reply, my front door opened.

A man in a green delivery uniform walked cautiously into my living room and placed a large pot of lilies on the dining room table. Then he gave a respectful nod and backed from the room, easing the door shut behind him.

I stared at the lilies as Jerome spoke and tried to work my way over to them so I could read the little white card that was attached. But the phone cord was too short.

"I can't hang up," Jerome said. "Someone's got to witness this cruelty. I'm sorry it has to be you. But I don't have that many friends left."

I caught a glimpse of myself in the hallway mirror as I moved back toward the kitchen. There were daubs of flour on my neck and chin. My left ear was white and there were pale blotches on my arms as well. God, I thought, I look like a leper. I remembered photographs of lepers in a *National Geographic* I'd seen as a child. The lepers looked doomed—participants in a ritual which left them no choice but to stumble from one rude hut to the next in search of shelter and companionship. As children we'd even played a game called Lepers. One person had to be the leper and tried to touch the others who ran away. The article described how the lepers had to eat apart from the healthy members of the tribe. Lepers were often removed to remote areas, where they were photographed with their bony arms extended—whether to display their ulcerated skin or toward some longed-for embrace, was not revealed.

"Are you going to hang up on me?" Jerome asked. "What do you know about having to borrow money and to beg for things you need? Go ahead; hang up. Live in comfort and peace and forget about your friend."

"Jerome, I always listen. I do what I can," I said. I was used to these attempts to force me to abandon him. When that failed he would try to make me feel guilty because my fortunate circumstances separated me from the uncertainty he suffered daily. "Try to be a little more normal, Jerome," I pleaded. "Try to understand that the world is a busy place, that the world—" But before I could finish he was shouting.

"I'm not normal! This is Jerome and I'm not normal. I'll never be normal!" he cried.

I held the receiver away from my ear and felt the scald of his words ripple over me. He was right, and no amount of pacifying and reassuring could cover up that truth—indeed the very truth I loved him for.

"Hurry up! Get off the phone, will you?" my husband called from inside the darkroom. Sometimes when I was talking to Jerome he would turn the radio on full blast. This time he contented himself with running the faucets and rattling things in his sink.

As I worked out the pie dough and listened to Jerome's distraught voice, I remembered the Jerome I'd met fifteen years ago, the Jerome who'd taken me to a deserted warehouse one night to show me his latest creation. He'd flicked a switch that ignited a row of lightbulbs suspended down the center of the high-ceilinged space. There, miraculously floating, dozens of feathers clung as if to the air itself. On closer inspection I saw that the feathers were attached to nylon fishing line strung from the ceiling. At the center of each feather cluster was a metal nub.

"Magnets," Jerome said proudly. "Watch this." Then he switched on a fan and all the feathers began to blow in exactly the same direction, holding their course as if by some strong unseen force that synchronized their motions.

"They're set to magnetic north," Jerome explained. He moved the fan around the room, but the feathers inevitably stabilized toward the same direction—magnetic north. I understood then that Jerome, like these feathers holding formation in an otherwise empty warehouse, took his marching orders from somewhere as far off and crucially situated as magnetic north itself. Yet only after I'd gone to the dictionary and looked up these words did I perceive their full import as regards my friend—that magnetic north was in fact nearly impossible to locate if another magnetic field was to come into the proximity of the compass needle. So it was for Jerome—a man easily pulled off course, sent twirling and plummeting earthward at the smallest gust of wind.

"Stop arguing against yourself and listen," I said sternly into the receiver. "Suppose Catlin is mistreating you. Suppose he wants you hanging there by your thumbs as you suspect, sick at heart, humiliated, waiting for him to call you."

"Okay," Jerome said in a small voice, satisfied that at last I was going to hear him out.

"Supposing," I said. "Supposing all that's true. What should I *do?*"

Jerome seemed to consider a moment, as if *doing* were the last thing on his mind. "Just tell me Catlin doesn't mean it," he said at last. "Tell me he's had an emergency. His dog died. He's ruptured a disc. Anything. But don't let me believe he's treating me this way on purpose."

Someone began to pound on the door again. My husband cursed and thumped about in the small space of the darkroom, but did not venture out. I was afraid, for Jerome's sake, to put the phone down. Then the door opened and two men in coveralls entered. One was carrying a small pine tree and the other had a spray of gladioli and a pot of lavender mums. A white satin ribbon hung down from the mums across the man's arm. The gold lettering read BELOVED MOTHER. The men placed the flowers and the tree near the lilies and turned to leave, but at the front door one of the men paused, gave a quick tug at the bill on his cap. They didn't even have a chance to close the door when a heavyset woman moved tentatively into the living room. She saw that I was on the telephone and placed an index finger over her lips as she tiptoed toward me into the kitchen. She was carrying a covered casserole dish.

"You must be Treena's daughter," she said and approached to give me a little peck on the cheek. She set the dish on the counter, patted me on the shoulder, then broke into muffled sobs. "I can't stay. Harold's in the car. God bless you," the woman said, wiping her eyes on her sleeve. Then she retraced her steps toward the door.

"There must be some mistake," I said.

"I'm tired of mistakes," Jerome said. "Nobody takes life seriously anymore. Look at the injury it does. Excuse-me-excuse-me! It's a litany from morning till night."

"I'm in the middle of somebody's funeral," I said aloud.

"Don't toy with me," Jerome said. "Don't mock me."

"I'm not mocking you. I'm your friend. I don't know why I am, but I am," I said.

"Some friend!" came my husband's muffled voice from the darkroom.

The sweet odor of flowers had begun to fill the living room. Now it drifted into the kitchen, where I was about to move the pie crust into the pan. I maneuvered the dough with both hands, holding the telephone receiver to my shoulder with my ear. Jerome wasn't talking, but I knew he was still there. I felt him there. As I looked up from the pie, I saw that a light fog was beginning to drift in from the bay along the shore. The pounding next door had stopped altogether now, but the memory of it was there like an undercurrent as I gazed out toward the bay.

"Jerome?" I said. But he didn't answer. "Jerome?" I repeated. I held the receiver and listened. As I waited I rested my gaze on the shoreline. The fog was lifting. Then, through the light-filled haze, I saw horses, a small band of them. They were riderless yet intent, as if someone or something was guiding them, urging them forward. The lead horse plunged without hesitation into the surf and began to swim toward a small island a few miles away. The other horses followed and I could only press the receiver against my neck in amazement and watch. There, on a beach where neither dog nor child ran free, a band of horses had clattered over stones, over sand, and into the waves. I put the receiver down on the counter and moved into the dining room to where the binoculars lay on the table near the lilies. I raised the glasses to my eyes. Striving above the waves I saw the heads of the horses. I could not take my eyes from them.

"What's this? What's going on here?" my husband demanded. "Is this some kind of bad joke?" he asked. I knew he was talking about the flowers. He went into the kitchen, and I heard him lift the lid on the casserole.

Through a break in the fog I could still see the horses. For a moment I imagined I could feel the steady pull of their legs in the current. Waves broke across my chest. I could see land in the distance like a thin silver streamer on the water.

I heard a click as my husband dropped the receiver into its cradle. Jerome, I thought with a leap of regret. But then I stood and listened as if our hold on each other had nothing to do with telephones, as if Jerome's silence still questioned, implored me to hold a course for him in the tumult and battering of the waves. My husband opened a drawer and I heard the clink of silverware.

"At least that damned pounding has stopped," he said. "It was driving me nuts. What a day!"

I held my gaze on the horses. I felt possessed of a surety, a strength that surprised me. Even my long hair seemed infused with an energy of its own as it flowed down my back. I was sure that if I were to take a boat to the island tomorrow, I would find hoofprints along the beach. They would have arrived, obedient to whatever instinct or necessity had drawn them there. And my friend Jerome, he too had an uncanny fidelity for destinations of which I was often the baffled lodestar.

I lowered the binoculars and turned toward my husband. He was at the table helping himself to the casserole. His spoon scraped the sides of the dish. The overpowering sweet scent of lilies made an invisible current in the room, and although they seemed to indicate a sadness for which I could do nothing, I leaned over and took a breath from their fragrance.

My husband lifted food to his mouth. As I sat down at the far end of the table, he looked up in such a way that I remembered the flour on my brow and neck. But he said nothing and looked at his plate again, as if thinking. Then he looked up and smiled with the fondness of one who endures much for the sake of a few moments' peace.

I saw that the fog had begun to move in around the house. We could be anywhere, I thought. Anywhere. But we were here. I held out my hand as he offered me my plate.

Them cute kinds ain't saloons.

Creatures

Elna had once said that beautifying was nothing more than grabbing Mother Nature by the throat and showing her who was boss. When Shelly arrived for her appointment, her friend was vigorously at work on an alabaster-complexioned teenager. Testimonies of terse, coiled ringlets spiraled past the girl's ears and down the back of her neck.

"Hey-there!" Elna called as Shelly settled into a chair across from what they laughingly called the hot seat.

"Where's your cat population?" Shelly asked. She unbuttoned her coat and slipped it onto the back of the chair. Elna's cats were a quick barometer for the household's travail now that Elna's marriage was in trouble. No matter in what state she arrived, Shelly always felt strangely cheered by the prospect of Elna's troubles—maybe because they were harder to solve than her own.

When Elna and Eugene had tried to split up the previous year, the clients had commiserated with Elna, said she was "doing the right thing," that Eugene was "only along for the ride," et cetera. But in the end, Elna had let him stay and her clients now kept their opinions to themselves.

This time around, Eugene was calling the shots. The day after New Year's he'd announced he was moving out, but not until spring, when an apartment he wanted would come available. Elna had complained so bitterly about the marriage that her friends were astonished she'd agreed to this. But theory had it Eugene might settle more congenially if she did things his way. Shelly knew it was harder for Elna to let the marriage go, now that Eugene was the one heading for the door. Still, things had been building up.

In the months prior to their current situation Eugene had been giving all the signs of a man having an affair—late nights, strange excuses. Once he'd even called Elna to say the gold cap on his front tooth had fallen into a load of gravel. It would be a while. Another time he'd phoned from a training session in a nearby town. He'd been learning to install a new kind of insulation. The afternoon meeting was supposed to allow him to come home that night, but he'd called Elna with a change of plans. His hemorrhoids were bothering him. They were so bad, he said he couldn't make the two-hour drive home. He'd have to spend the night there alone, in pain. He was sorry. He was having to stand up while making this very call, he said, an odd catch in his voice. Elna's friends said it didn't sound like your regular excuse. He'd also started bringing home single rosebuds wrapped in cellophane from the supermarket. Out of the blue, he'd call Elna from a pay phone to say, "Hi, honey, just wanted you to know I love you."

It had been hard for Elna to believe Eugene had somebody on the side—even harder to admit, once she believed it. Shelly had been all too willing to confirm the diagnosis. She'd had her own experiences with cheating men. She'd been glad to share with Elna an article in a women's magazine that told all the signs. "Constant irritability and fault-finding"—those were two they'd agreed especially fit Eugene.

As she settled herself in her chair, Shelly continued to scan the shop for the cats. When she didn't see them, she called to them by name. Elna, who'd been methodically swiveling the curling rod to the teenager's head, withdrew it and stepped over to Shelly. She bent and, in a confidential tone, said, "Honey—Lucky and Lightning are no longer with us. They've gone where all good, but sadly flawed creatures go." Then she retreated to her client, having seemingly dispensed with a very unpleasant matter.

Clearly things had taken a desperate turn. Shelly consoled herself, noticing that the remaining young black cat, Veronica, was basking in the last rays of afternoon sunlight. She nudged the cat with the toe of her shoe, and its eyes blinked open and shut several times, as if completing some coded message from a dream-filled interior.

"I wish I could have gone with them, straight to kitty heaven," Elna was saying. "Do not pass Safeway or Twelve-Star Video. One minute the needle, then poof! Heaven."

The idea of heaven had always eluded Shelly, and, linked to "kitty," the word only revived images of the two missing cats, stranded in some lonely outpost of the mind. They had been fixtures the ten years she'd been coming to the shop, always curled in one chair or another. Each time a client uprooted them they would tolerantly resituate themselves.

Lightning, a huge white cat with a streak of black down one side, was forever inviting himself into a client's lap and having to be scolded down. The other, Lucky, a tea-colored part Siamese, was like the sleep of the world. She had once crawled into the clothes dryer for a nap and managed to endure several minutes on Knits / Gentle / Low with a load of bikini panties. "If she'd been on Cottons she'd be looking *up* to the mice," Elna had quipped. She'd been affectionate about even the failures of her cats. It was hard to believe she'd had them put to sleep.

Recently Shelly had heard on a talk show that willful deaths or injuries to innocent pets often signaled a worsening of relationships between their owners. Elna leaned against the mirror that ran the length of the room and appraised the rather glum-looking teenager undergoing transformation. She used a comb to tease a fringe of bangs onto the girl's forehead as she continued. "Lucky, with her own little motorized tongue, licked down an entire cube of butter, then did her job in my yarn basket. *One* of the clinchers," Elna said. "They just got too old." Shelly didn't contradict her friend, though she suspected age had nothing to do with it.

"Veronica, you lucky devil," Shelly said conspiratorially to the remaining cat, "to be young and in control of your functions—house-trained like the rest of us."

Shelly had been feeling the closest thing to joy in a long time when she'd entered the shop. She hadn't been prepared to hear about the disposal of Elna's cats, and was dismayed at how suddenly any relief in life could be so quickly burdened again with sadness. Her eighty-year-old mother had gone through a diagnostic test that afternoon which had taken longer than expected. During the test, Shelly had sat with a magazine on her lap, imagining the long thin probe being worked into her mother's stomach and upper intestines while the doctor's eye searched for the reason she had been bleeding. Shelly had mentally entered that darkness as a small wink of light, grazing and scraping the deep interior. The trouble with the imagination, she thought, was that the mind could go anywhere, so you could never tell from one moment to the next where you might end up.

The doctor had prepared Shelly and her mother to deal with stomach cancer or ulcers, but miraculously nothing had been found. She had come to her hair appointment prepared to celebrate her mother's good fortune. But the deaths of the cats had changed all that.

"Oh, honey, we were just bawling our eyes out after I took them to the vet's. My clients sat in their chairs and cried, and I blubbered right along with them," Elna said, bending to the teenager. "Cousin Flo came over on her lunch break to say good-bye to them. Then I closed those poor babies into the same cardboard carrier and drove them to the clinic."

To be shut into a small dark space against your will was one of the most frightening things Shelly could imagine. Her mind veered out of the box with its doomed cats and back toward her friend. Shelly could see Elna didn't know at all how to represent what she'd done. She was alternately hot and cold over it—pitying the cats while trying to justify her part in their fate.

The bells on the shop door jangled and Gretchen, Elna's daughter, entered with her two children. Her face looked puffy to Shelly, like a person who'd been either hit in the face or crying, or both. "I need some of your magic hair spray, Mom," Gretchen announced. She picked peppermint candies for her children from the fishbowl which had been converted to a candy dish after the fish were found floating belly-up one morning. "Hey, it's like a funeral in here."

"If you only knew, dear," Elna said.

"She *offed* Lucky and Lightning," said the teenager, like the surviving member of a Greek chorus.

Gretchen made a sound deep in her throat—an eruption that sprang from the unpredictableness of human utterance itself.

"I can't believe you did that, Mom," Gretchen said, holding her children by their jacket collars to keep them from taking another step toward their grandmother.

"I suppose I could have just let them scramble for it outside," Elna said, ignoring her. "But I would have been worrying all the time. Besides, it's cold out there, and if something chased them—"

"My cat sleeps with me," said the teenager, a beacon of ruthless insinuation.

"Lightning slept with me, too," Elna said quietly, making clear that intimacy could not have staved off the inevitable. "The last straw was him spraying down the floor vent. We breathed cat piss for a week. I dumped cologne, Purex, baby powder, a bottle of cedar scent down it—even got back into my hippie days and burned incense."

With the cats gone, the shop felt larger, less cozy. Shelly noticed Veronica had moved to the back of a chair at the window, one paw V-ing the Venetian blind where she gazed into the yard. "She's looking for them," Elna said. "She can't imagine what's keeping them, thank God. Lucky and Lightning," she mused, "forever expected in Veronica's cat mind."

"We didn't even have a funeral," Gretchen said plaintively.

"Flo and I thought about going sentimental, burying them in the backyard with two little stone markers from one of those catalogs, but I chickened out," Elna said. "No—they just went into the incinerator. 'Cremate them,' I told the vet, 'and do whatever you do—I mean, when no one takes whatever's left.' "

At the mention of the backyard, Gretchen's children wriggled from her and eased out the shop entrance. Shelly wished, for a moment, she could go with them. She knew Elna made light of things when she felt them most, that she would be cryptic with bursts of admission until she had eroded some kind of invisible barrier between her actions and her feelings.

"Honestly," Elna said, "Lucky would sashay in from the great outdoors, stand right up against the door she'd just walked through, lift her leg, and spray, right in front of me!"

"I didn't know female cats lifted their legs," Shelly said.

"This one did. Lifted it just like a tom, smart as you please, and shot her tank, then pranced off like she'd accomplished something."

"Little did she know," Gretchen said.

"You bet," Elna said, with muscle in her voice. "The Kevorkian of cats had called her number." It was five o'clock. Elna walked over and closed the Venetian blinds. "Open them, shut them. Who cares?" Elna said. She returned to the girl in the swivel chair and rotated her toward the mirror.

Elna's swiveling of the chair, then stopping it, steadied

everything for a moment. With the blinds closed, the eyes of the shop seemed closed, and Shelly felt the particular intimacy of women alone in a room, talking, trading confidences, speaking their minds.

"Kimberly's wearing forest green to the prom," Elna said, her voice rubbing the consonants in "forest green." The ebony of trees at dusk entered Shelly's mind—a pungent, under-boughs' darkness that overpowered the smell of hair spray mingled with cat urine. She imagined night falling in the forests on the mountains behind the town, the creatures alive there, able to survive nights and days in snow and rain, searching for food, for shelter.

A strong draft ran through the shop as Gretchen's children burst into the room again. "Stay inside, please, children, or stay out," Elna said. Shelly realized eerily that Elna was using the same tone with the children she'd used with the missing cats. The children had just dropped to their knees in the middle of the floor with the black cat when the shop door suddenly opened and Eugene entered. He veered around the children and, without a glance, shot past everyone into the kitchen.

"Brace yourself," Elna said with a knowing look.

"Mom, okay if I make a long-distance call?" Gretchen asked, seizing the moment. "It's about a job. They shut off my phone." Shelly saw Elna go into her stoic helpful-against-the-odds mode.

"Use the kitchen phone," Elna said, "but make it snappy."

Shelly could feel how stretched beyond limits Elna was because of Gretchen, yet she knew Elna would likely do a lifetime of setting aside her own boundaries for her daughter. Shelly hated her friend's helplessness, but she also took pity and even admired her, because at least helplessness meant you were out there in the deep water, risking things. Her friend lived somehow beyond the prudent, fix-it mentality of others she knew. For Elna things were patently wrong, and they were going farther in that direction, no matter what Shelly or anyone wished for her. She tried to imagine a life where Elna wouldn't be burdened and ensnared, but no matter what she considered, no likely solution occurred.

Soon Gretchen's laughter drifted through the open door to the kitchen. She was always "looking for a job" or "about to get a job." In this, it struck Shelly, she wasn't so different from Eugene. After a few minutes the register of her voice changed and she could be heard talking to Eugene. Her tone was placating, the way someone used to calamity tries to soothe away consequences.

"All that room out there!" Eugene blurted. "All that ocean and forest, and she has to ram a goddamn California lawyer with two kids in a goddamn camper." On the way into the house, Eugene had spotted a dent Gretchen had left in his pickup. Elna stopped what she was doing to listen.

"Why not ram the ocean? Something with a little give-and-take," Eugene cried at the top of his voice. "Aim for an oil tanker, be ambitious—a raft of logs, a fishing trawler. Give chaos a chance!" he ranted.

"Eugene's off his spool again," Elna said, a high ripple in her voice meant to counter his tirade by seeming to indicate the malfunction of an ordinary household appliance. Eugene had always claimed that Gretchen's problems, her sudden incursions on his and Elna's lives, her bad choices in men, two children by an absent father—these ongoing pressures had made it impossible for him and Elna. To a certain extent, Shelly thought he was right. Whatever faults Eugene had, no one could dispute the fact that he'd been an absolute natural, a veritable blue-ribbon champion at living with things in a mess. He re-entered the beauty shop now, drawn backward by some invisible force centered in Elna.

"You never asked *me*," he said to the company at large, his back to Elna. "The queen of demolition derbies, and you loan her my truck like loaning a can opener."

"My God, Gene, it's only a dent," Elna said, hardly grazing his attention.

"I can't get over it," he said. "Snuff the cats. Ram the truck. I'm lucky to have a door to walk through." He hitched his jeans and ducked to look at himself in the mirror. His black hair roiled in a glistening wave he pushed back from his forehead.

Shelly noticed Eugene had dark circles under his eyes and he'd lost weight. So had Elna, for that matter. She'd always been wasp-waisted, but now her skin seemed oddly transparent, as if everything inside, the entire circuitry of her body, were visible to whoever came within her parameters. Eugene disappeared into the kitchen.

Elna spun the prom girl toward her and gave her a hand mirror so she could see the back of her head. "Mister Righteous," Elna said. " 'Honey, honey,' he'd say— 'there's a mess in here. You might want to check it out.' Well, I checked it out all right!"

The prom girl stared into the mirror, adrift on the small bright raft of her face in a shark-infested sea. She bobbed her head, and the drooling curls danced briefly.

Meanwhile Gretchen's children had forced the surviving cat under the nail-polishing table. Shelly had the all-encompassing sensation that places of refuge were thinning out across the face of the planet. Soon enough, if a human impulse fixed its mark on a creature, it would be found and destroyed. There could be delay, but no lasting retreat. Maybe it had always been this way and she was just now realizing it.

"You're going to look amazing in that forest green," Elna said to the teenager. "If that boy was shy before, he's going to be speechless now." The girl frowned and pulled at the neck of her T-shirt. It was clear the shirt wouldn't lift easily over her hairdo.

"Is that expendable?" Elna asked.

"I guess so," the girl said vaguely.

"Darlin', you'd be surprised what's expendable by the time you get my age." Elna reached into a drawer and took out a pair of scissors.

"I still don't see how you did what you did, Mom," Gretchen said, reentering from the kitchen. She was speaking to her mother in the mirror. "Just because you and Gene aren't making it. We had those cats fifteen years," she said. "You're mean. Just plain mean!" Shelly could tell her friend was carefully not letting herself be provoked.

Elna took the scissors and began a vertical cut from the girl's neckline between the hints of her breasts. The scissors snipped viciously in the silence of the beauty shop. When she finished, she dropped them into the drawer, then slid it shut with a decisive thud.

From the kitchen a loud cascading of pans sounded. Eugene swore and Shelly looked up to see him pace past the doorway. He returned to stare briefly at the women in the shop, then broke away into the kitchen again, having evidently collected fresh energy from just glancing at them.

Child voices murmured from under the table. Shelly felt an undercurrent in the room, as when messages and secrets are being exchanged. She remembered what it was to be a child, crawling into the musky darkness under beds and tables, able to hear everything that went on; being there, yet not there. Once a pan of grease on the stove had caught fire while she'd been exploring the space under her parents' bed. Her mother had run through the rooms carrying the flaming pan, yelling "Fire!" and calling for her in a tone of ultimate panic, which changed to fury when she eventually discovered her under the bed. To this day, Shelly instinctively connected certain states of anxiety and threat with fire.

"Things are going to change around here," Elna said. "I see to everything else, and I'm seeing to that. There you go, dear," she said to Kimberly. Elna helped her lift the T-shirt over her head through the rough slit. The girl sat uneasily a moment in her bra until Gretchen reached into the little side room where her mother mixed hair colors and handed her a flannel shirt.

"Kimberly's going to dress in my bedroom," Elna said. "I told her I'd do her hair for free just to see her in her dress." Kimberly slipped on the shirt and moved toward the kitchen on her way to the bedroom to dress.

A mournful howl came from the cat, then giggling from the children. Their legs spidered from under the frilly table. "Jo-Jo, come out!" Gretchen called to her son. When he didn't appear she pulled him forth like a wheelbarrow by his legs.

"After what she did, I'm scared to leave my kids with her," Gretchen said. She took up a comb from the counter and raked it across her son's scalp. Gretchen's daughter approached Elna's work area clutching the glaring cat by its middle.

Shelly was used to the charade of Gretchen and her mother fighting over the children. She'd been in the shop once when Elna had called the Children's Protective Services, threatening to take them away. But since Gretchen left her children with Elna most of the time anyway, the threat was empty.

"When I was pregnant with her," Elna once told Shelly, "if I'd known the trouble I was in for, I'd have climbed onto the roof and dashed myself to the pavement like a watermelon."

Kimberly slowly eased into the doorway from the kitchen. Everyone had turned to look. Eugene was visible over one bare shoulder in the fluorescent light. Gretchen pulled at one of the small gold rings in her nose and, with her eyes on the girl, sat down under a dryer that was cocked open near Shelly.

The girl rustled forward, leaving a cool tracing of air in her wake. The taffeta sheen of the dress dimpled with dark whispering pools as she glided toward them and turned, her arms lightly at her sides. Like a calm fir tree in their clearing, she stood for a moment, then began again to turn, slowly, like someone in the vortex of a dream.

Suddenly the black cat let out a long, involuntary moan. It struggled free of the child's grasp and leaped precariously onto the swivel chair. Before they realized what was happening, the cat was midair in a short unwieldy arc toward the girl's bare shoulders. Its claws sank into the pure fleshy center of the room. The girl gave a raw cry of pain. If an eagle had dropped onto her shoulder to lift her from earth, she might have given such a cry. Poised, electric, the cat stared violently at them from its human perch.

Elna rushed forward with her face turned away, like a woman about to handle fire. She caught the cat by its fur and flung it from the girl's shoulders against the mirror. For a moment the animal appeared to be leaping out of itself, multiplied, quenched and resurrected at once as it rippled along the counter, then became airborne again, clearing the fishbowl before it dropped to the floor and streaked past their ankles. The girl began to shudder, then to sob openly, holding on to herself.

Shelly moved to catch Elna firmly by the shoulders. "There," Shelly said as she held her. "There." She took Elna's helpless blows against her back until they subsided. The cat had made its escape through the kitchen. Shelly imagined it tunneling into the farthest recesses of the house.

When Elna broke free and turned to the others, it was clear she'd crossed some boundary from which she looked back at them like one who holds a territory beyond challenge. Everyone in the room balanced unsteadily on the rim of the moment. A switch had somehow been thrown in all their heads at once. Night had fallen suddenly in their clearing. Each of them gazed warily out of the darkness at the others with the lime-green eyes of the young black cat, a creature forced to its limits and past.

There was unearthly calm and stillness in the space they now inhabited. They seemed suspended in the close chemical smell of the room, but elsewhere in the house they heard things falling, glassware shattering—the racing, desperate plunge of an animal seeking its full measure of darkness.

Shelly stared at her friend and realized she didn't know what Elna might do next—that everything, and everyone, had somehow been reduced to their simplest, most destructible element. She was aware that her childhood dread of fire was unreasonably alive in her. Whatever was flammable in the room rose to make itself known all at once—the nylon flounce along the mirror, cans of hair spray, raw clumps of hair at the base of the swivel chair, cellophane glinting from a wastebasket, hair again, the very hair on her head. The hair on all their heads. A woman with a pan of fire seemed to be running through her mind, fanning oxygen into flames, igniting whatever she passed. Shelly knew she and the others had arrived at some precarious boundary—where, despite their strongest instincts, they seemed to have agreed that no one would run from this room.

At seventy-four she said, "I would rather play poker with five or six experts than eat." —POKER ALICE

She

Who

Is

Untouched

by

Fire

"The soul may be the part of you that sees the dream."
JOHN NANCE, *The Tasaday Soul*

Waking up and looking to the other side of the bed, seeing no one there, wondering to herself without herself, *Where's Georgia?* Thinking, *She must be upstairs already.*

Raising herself up and out of bed, but wholly inside the question. Upstairs to the rocker, thinking: *usually here by the stove.* Next, with an anxiousness high in her chest—*Georgia not where she sits, not sitting there!*

Downstairs, into the spare bedroom—*No sign of her.* High ripple of panic, into her bedroom, looking again to her own bed. Looking for Georgia. To stand at the foot of the rumpled bed from which she had just arisen. To stare: empty.

Slowly, as she gazed, a calm began to settle on her. Everything was as it should be. Perhaps no one was missing. She marveled at the simplicity, the surety of it—as if memory itself had swooped down on her like a hawk and shaken her to herself in an instant. *She* was Georgia. That body of that name. Whoever it was, outside or inside her, that one who had been missing Georgia, had somehow been satisfied. The *searching for, the without—Georgia— anywhere* seemed to have revised itself against her disappearance. She could return. Could stay, for now.

Later she told everyone about the strange loss of herself. Told it as a visitor to her world, the world of Georgia. She didn't explain away the strangeness, the setting aside of herself in order to find herself. Rather, she was moved to tell it as if it were ordinary and unaccountable at once, a thing that could happen to anyone. Yet no one to whom she spoke admitted having had such an experience.

The more she encountered their bewildered listening, the more she puzzled at the difference of her experience. Who or what amalgamation had she been as she'd searched for herself? She'd had no consciousness of a "self." She was simply a *looking-for-Georgia*.

Who in the past, she wondered, had ever looked for Georgia? Her husband, now fourteen years dead? Certainly he'd looked for her in the house, called out to her each morning for forty years, waking on one side of the bed to find her on the other. It was he who'd usually gotten up first. Had some "looking" consciousness of her late husband entered her briefly—for the experience had lasted some ten minutes—and if so, *why* was he looking for her? Still, she'd had no actual sense of her husband—

no face, mind, or voice of him, as she'd searched, only the unattached question: *Where is Georgia?*

Not long after her disappearance she took her daughter into the spare bedroom. She said to her, "Here's the jade horse. I've fixed it," for one of its legs had been broken when her daughter had brought it home from China. Everything precious in the house had strangely begun to call attention to itself. "Take it with you," Georgia urged. She had the sense that her brief absence had divested her. It was initially refreshing, this letting go, but also as if everything she'd cherished began suddenly and vehemently to oppress her. When Georgia picked up the horse, the heft of green jade was cool to her hand. A hairline crack on one of the forelegs showed where it had been mended. But her daughter drew back. Georgia saw that this emptying out, this downdraft of eagerness which expressed itself as an impulse to shed her possessions, seemed to frighten others.

"No," the daughter said. "I might break it carrying it home. Anyway, you aren't going anywhere."

"Don't be so sure about that," her mother said, and she was aware of her smile as she smiled it, a strange, knowing smile, for she had already been *somewhere.* She had been missing to herself in her very body, and even as she missed herself, she had searched for Georgia inside the no-one-here. She saw her daughter as if from a great distance as she moved to leave. For a wistful, glancing instant she wanted to kiss her daughter's cheek, a thing she never did.

As she let others witness her lostness from herself in that former time, she became other than herself, wider in her perspective somehow. She caressed the fact of her return. Slowly she had leaked back into the consciousness of someone called Georgia—someone who now was different from everyone else she spoke to, someone who had been "away" and strangely intimate with her absence, as if she'd been searched out in her habitat and called forth. How easily she put aside the idea of her husband as the looking-for-Georgia-one! That was an idea, *one* idea. She could have it and set it aside.

Some unattached knowing had unknown her inside her own flesh, then reinfused her so that Georgia was both inside and outside her now. She felt tender toward this one she carried upstairs and down, this Georgia who could tell the story of being searched for, then of being given back into herself as the one known as Georgia. Yet she had returned with a puzzled gazing-out at them as they listened, as they proposed a range of familiar possibilities—sleepwalking, out-of-body travel, the start of Alzheimer's, a light stroke, an embolism, daydreaming. She listened. Said nothing, either to confirm or deny. She fortified her disappearance with a ransom of silence.

When others spoke of what had happened to her, she felt led away from an important site of recognition for which she had no language, and theirs carried her far afield, did not apply. She took pity on their attempts to mollify the outward surfaces of her unaccountable disappearance and her even more miraculous return. It was as if she had walked through fire, yet no bodily sign of her experience had marked her.

Georgia, she said to herself as she carried herself to the roadway and began to walk, to gaze around her and to think *Georgia* and *not-Georgia* into the things she passed. A blush of pleasure rose inside her, and she could hear a voice both inside and out, calling to her, asking calmly: *Georgia, what are you doing? Where are you going?*

I was rock, dark rock
and the parting was violent. . . .

—PABLO NERUDA

A

Box

of

Rocks

Arlen gazed out the bedroom window facing onto the pasture and saw Elida as she passed in silhouette over the ridge. He went to the bed, sat down and pulled on his socks, then slipped into his trousers and shirt. He returned to the window in time to see his wife reemerge, almost as if she had climbed out of the earth itself. The only acknowledgment she'd made toward the cold was a light jacket and a head scarf.

In the half-light he could see she was carrying something, but he couldn't make out what. Her shoulders were drawn forward, and she looked old to him, though she wasn't yet thirty.

Arlen had been in love with Elida since she was fifteen, had chosen her over her sister Dory, whom he had fancied briefly. There had been something too sudden and elusive about Dory. "A girl made for tragedy," his mother had warned, and after that he could not look at Dory without feeling that her life did not belong to her.

Only once before had Arlen seen his wife locked obsessively to an action, and that had been two years after their marriage. They'd learned Elida would be unable either to conceive or to carry a child. The situation couldn't be reversed, they were told. They had considered adopting a child and had even begun the proceedings. Then Arlen had lost his job delivering oil for a company that had fallen on hard times. The agency advised them that their case would be reexamined at a later date, since the lack of a steady income made the couple ineligible.

It was then Elida had begun to raise ducks. Arlen had persevered with her, even though the ducks were messy and the noise they made got on his nerves. One day Arlen found his wife holding a sickly duckling at the kitchen table, forcing water down its throat with a medicine dropper. Its eyes were hooded, its head drooping. Elida had asked him to hold it while she continued to drop water into its throat. When they'd succeeded in reviving the bird, he'd felt joy with her at having been a part of another creature's survival.

After the ducks had attained some size, he would see her followed by a line of them across the field. They joined her whenever she left the house and made her the point of their arrow. She had delighted at each stage of their development, especially the day she'd watched them begin to swim in the pond near the house.

One morning she and Arlen had come out of the house and discovered a clump of feathers on the porch. More feathers were caught in the chicken wire around the pen, as if forced there by a fierce wind. Inside the pen were the grisly remains of the ducks. The scene looked to Arlen like the afterbirth of some creature he could not fully imagine. Elida sat around the house for several days, turning away food, talking little.

A letter from Dory in Kansas City arrived during this time with an unexpected request. Dory had written that since her husband had left she'd had to get a job. She could no longer manage her child alone, a little girl named Elmi whom Arlen and Elida had never seen.

Dory's husband had traveled for a company that sold fencing. The relatives had taken one look at her salesman husband and said that Dory ought to use one of the fences on him. Dory might have had some of these feelings herself. Whatever the reason, she'd taken their child and gone on the road with her husband. Though the relatives said Dory had smartened up, her vigilance hadn't saved the marriage. Her husband had left their hotel one night in Saint Louis, saying he was going to gas up the car for the next morning's drive, but he had not returned.

Dory's letter asked Arlen and Elida to take on the raising of Elmi. It had been no surprise that Dory's marriage had ended, but they'd never expected to become involved in this important way. Dory said she would send checks to help with the girl's care so it wouldn't be a financial burden. She thought the child would be better off with Arlen and Elida, there in the country, and even though she was two hundred miles away, she said she would try to come on the bus to see her as often as she could.

UNTIL TWO weeks ago the child, Elmi, had been living with them. They'd kept her for three years. They had even celebrated her fifth birthday by planting five plum trees in the orchard. Dory had seldom visited, although she'd kept her word about sending money from her paychecks. She had acted as if her daughter would always stay with Arlen and Elida. It had been easy for them to believe Elmi would never leave them.

Shortly after the child's fifth birthday, Dory had remarried. This time she'd found a man of some means. Her circumstances were so much better she'd decided she wanted her daughter with her again. She announced in a recent letter that she would, in fact, be coming to get Elmi. Would they please write to let her know when would be convenient.

"We won't answer," Elida had said, as she'd lifted the lid of the woodstove and dropped the letter into the fire. After that they would catch themselves looking at the red-haired child as if she were a photograph of a child running, or laughing, or sleeping. At these times Arlen would feel her preciousness to him so fiercely it would sweep over him like an invisible wave that forced him downward into its undertow. The bleakness of the feeling seemed a preparation for what was coming, as though the pain were being pulsed into him in minutely bearable doses.

On his way outside to see what his wife was doing on the ridge, Arlen automatically glanced into the child's room. Elida had arranged the stuffed toys on the bed as Elmi had liked to find them before bedtime. The child's clothes hung neatly in the open closet. The room itself seemed to accuse him, to ask what kind of protector he was if he had allowed its inhabitant to be taken from it.

"Elida," he called, when he saw his wife moving downhill. Only when she'd dropped what she'd been carrying did he see it was stones of all sizes and shapes. She was piling them near the swing set he'd built for Elmi. The rocks were heaped onto a scuffed patch of ground where the child's feet had touched down each time she'd given herself a boost into the air.

"I want you to build me something," Elida said when he reached her. He glanced to where she was looking. Some of the rocks were the size of a fist. Others could be carried in a pocket, and still others were as big as a cantaloupe or a person's head.

"What's this going to do? What good's this going to do?" Arlen said. He bent down and picked up one of the rocks. There was frost on it and it was damp on the side that had touched the ground. He brought it close to his face. The smell of dirt still clung to it. The cold coming from the stone was like a small intimate engine whose workings were hidden.

The sun had come up and the frost on the other stones was starting to melt. They glistened and their colors deepened. He could see which were moss green or slate-colored. Others had bright flecks of fool's gold or were speckled like a bird's egg.

"She can't have it all her way," Elida said. She took several coin-sized stones from her jacket pocket and let them clatter onto the others. Arlen could see there was no reasoning with her. He went to the shed and got the hammer and handsaw, some nails and a few rough boards. Then he set to work.

At the end of the morning she came to see what he'd done. The box was nearly finished. He'd fashioned a lid that could be nailed on, once the box was filled. The hammer blows made a bright definitive sound as he tapped in the last nail. Elida ran her hands inside the space as if to take its dimensions fully into herself.

ON THE day Dory had come to take Elmi, the sheriff was at the house when Arlen returned from town. The lawman had gone inside by the time Arlen had parked the truck. For a moment Arlen stood beside the truck, taking in the scene. Then he moved to pass Dory where she leaned with a deputy against the sheriff's car just outside the gate.

"You got my letter, Arlen G.," Dory said to him. "Don't pretend you didn't."

"You just come on back," the deputy said, as Arlen moved past them. "You go in there and we'll never get this done." He tried to take hold of Arlen's arm but Arlen stepped aside and quickened his pace until he reached the house and climbed the steps.

When Arlen came into the living room, Elmi was kicking and screaming in the hold of the sheriff. He had thrown her across his shoulder, meaning to carry her out of the house. Elmi looked straight at Arlen, then pushed her face inside the man's collar and clamped her teeth into the sheriff's neck. The sheriff let out a string of curses and lost his hold on the child. Once she was free, Elmi seemed to realize that neither Arlen nor Elida could stop what was happening. She ran to Arlen long enough to grasp his pant leg before she made for her room and disappeared under the bed.

"Damn!" the sheriff swore, as he took his hand away from his neck. He left a thin streak of blood on khaki where he wiped his trousers. He scowled at Arlen and walked past him out the front door and onto the porch.

Arlen saw Elida braced against the living room wall. A deadness had come into her eyes that made him want to throw something, anything; to pick up his easy chair or the entire dish cabinet and hurl it. He had that kind of energy. Crazy energy. But he didn't want these to be Elmi's last memories. So he stood still as the wildness rippled through his shoulders and upper thighs. With the front door open, he could see the sheriff go over to Dory and the deputy. Then Dory headed for the house, with the sheriff behind her.

"She's my little girl and I aim to have her," Dory shouted loud enough for them to hear inside the house. Then Dory was in the room, striding past them and into Elmi's bedroom. The sheriff was close behind her.

"I'm not yours! I'm not a bit yours!" Elmi cried between bursts of wailing from under the bed. Dory got onto her knees and peered into the darkness under the child's bed.

"She has a right," the sheriff warned when Arlen moved as if to enter the child's room.

Arlen watched as Dory reached her entire upper body under the bed and took Elmi by the arm. Elmi gave a shrill cry, as if she had been caught in a snare. As Dory pulled the child into the light, Arlen felt Elida come to his side and put her hand on his arm. His forearm was tensed and flexing, as if he were lifting something. The sheriff stood between them and Dory and the child.

"Now see what you've done," Dory said to Elida. She stopped a moment in the bedroom doorway with the child pressed to her hip. Elida seemed unable to move or even to speak. Her eyes were searching the child for some way of holding to her beyond all this. Dory managed to lift Elmi, but was barely able to contain the struggling, wailing child. She and the sheriff moved toward the front door.

"You can do this, but that don't make it right," Arlen said to Dory as she swept past them with Elmi. But his words were drowned out by Elmi's inconsolable cries as she was carried down the steps. His whole body felt as if it were being funneled upward, against all nature, as in movies he'd seen of waterfalls run backward. He heard the sheriff tell his deputy to open the car doors.

"Settle down, honey," the sheriff said. From inside the car Elmi's cries seemed those of a small insistent bird as it is closed into the dark. The car doors slammed and they heard no more. Soon the car spun away down the gravel road.

Elmi had been gone a week when Dory wrote to tell Elida to pack the girl's clothing and toys and send them to her in Kansas City. She didn't ask; she told her. There had been "such a commotion," as Dory put it, that she'd come off without Elmi's things. "I paid for a lot of those things and Elmi needs them," she wrote. Dory said she would be glad to pay the postage once the package arrived.

ARLEN carried the box and lid he had built over to the pile of stones at the swing set and placed them on the ground. He put the hammer and a packet of nails beside it. Elida lifted the stones, one and two at a time, and began to drop them into the box. They made a blunted sound that fell back into itself as they struck the boards.

Arlen's body seemed to thicken with resolve as he watched the box fill. They had been unable to say much to each other, either to comfort or to ease the fact that the child was no longer with them. He began to bend, take up stones and drop them into the box. The child was gone. Alive, but gone from them, probably forever. Elida held the lid on as he hammered it shut. Their muscles strained as they lifted the box and carried it to the truck.

As if they had planned it, they climbed up and sat for a while on the truck bed with the box between them. A stillness rose from it that calmed and fortified them, as if something of the child's joyful presence lagged behind, something that had nothing to do with belonging. Finally Elida took a black marker, and wrote Dory's name and address onto the box. Then she eased herself down from the truck and walked back into the house.

When, after a week or two, no reply or reaction came from Dory, they were not surprised. It didn't matter whether they heard from her since there was no release for them from Elmi's absence.

After a few weeks Dory sent photos of Elmi, and later, notes about her progress, as if nothing had occurred between them. For a time this continued. Then even these communications dwindled and finally stopped altogether. Elida had made no reply to her sister, and Arlen hadn't interfered. Other relatives would pass along glimpses of the child from time to time, but it was like news of a ghost, the images faded as though not meant to last.

When anyone tried to soften the incident between the sisters or to move them back toward each other, Elida would withdraw. Arlen had watched her get up and leave the room more than once. After a while his own longing for the child seemed inexplicably to fall away. He hadn't asked anything for himself after the ordeal, even though he would have liked somehow for the photos to have continued to arrive, each one moving the girl a step farther away from him, yet closer in his imagining of her. They never spoke again of bringing another child into their lives.

Those who knew the situation had said that when Elmi got a mind of her own, she'd come back to them. These friends meant to comfort, but Arlen and Elida knew it was only what people said when things couldn't be changed or resolved. They knew that a child lives the life it is given, and that Elmi had been too young for their love to have left more than a trace of memories, in which they too were fading.

In the standoff between the sisters, Arlen was aware that Elida held the balance of power. It was Elida who had to be moved. But she had no intention of relenting and, as time passed, Arlen assumed more of her attitude than he sometimes realized.

In the twenty-five years that then passed, Elida's slow, wordless sorrow had become embedded in Arlen's own grief. He would have liked, in time, to have seen the break between the sisters mended. But time had all but run out. Elida was going down fast now. From the day they'd discovered the cancer, the doctor had given her six months and all but a month of that time was gone. So when a knock came at their door and Arlen opened it to find Dory standing there, his first impulse had strangely been relief.

Then his gaze fell on the bouquet of mums and carnations Dory cradled in her arms. He stared at the flowers, trying to catch hold of their meaning, the pungent smell of carnations working on him like an irritant.

He had been feeling both used up and rooted by the daily necessities of tending his wife. The memory of Elmi still ran like a river between them. Even after all this time, it was cool and mysteriously sustaining, could prick the heart unexpectedly and seep into the farthest reaches of his being, especially now that he was losing Elida. He felt the child had somehow been gathered back the way he had seen horses foraging in spring, finding the hidden tender shoots and pulling them deeply in.

"No, you can't see her," Arlen said. Then before Dory could hand him the flowers he closed the door. Dory's look of pained astonishment stayed in his mind long after he returned to Elida's bedside. He knew it would rise up in him when this time of watching after Elida had passed, and that he would wonder if he had done the right thing, even when there was no going back. His heart hadn't been hard when he'd turned her away, only sad, as if it were the only way he could handle the situation at the moment.

When he opened the door later he feared Dory might have left the flowers, but she had taken them with her. He'd worried about explaining them. He could shut a door, but throwing out flowers—that would somehow have been harder, away from what he'd meant. He had thought of telling Elida that her sister had come. That, at least, would have included her in his decision. But there was always the chance Elida might have objected to how he'd handled Dory. The more he played this out in his mind, the more he felt he should simply let it stand, and not trouble these last hours. Whatever happened, he would be the one who had to remember, and that would be punishment enough if, later, he felt he'd been wrong. One thing was clear. He had kept his wife from painful affairs that might have consumed and unsettled her when her life ought to be calm and in order. This was no time for Elida to have either a reunion or an argument with Dory.

He propped a photo, of Elmi taken in the swing, near the headboard where Elida could see it when she reached for her water glass. Elmi was a woman now. They'd heard she had children of her own, children they might have seen and known had the sisters relented. But over the years everything had become fixed, irrevocable, closed. And Arlen had, at last, taken his own part in this. But how strange it was, Arlen thought, that his heart could be completely without malice, yet allow him to do a thing others could see as cruel. If he stood away from himself, he saw that under different circumstances he would have embraced Dory and shown her to the bedside. But in the moment, his choice had somehow involved his loyalty to Elida and that pent-up time when Elmi had depended on him and he had done nothing. Closing the door to Dory had carried him far outside the reasonable wish to resolve one's differences whenever possible. It had been possible, but something had jammed in him and he'd had to trust it.

ARLEN had managed the immediate details of Elida's death with more ease than he managed the days he now spent alone. He seemed awash in time. Still, he'd become used to supplying Elida's view to the questions he'd had to answer. He was amazed at how naturally this occurred.

He'd known, for instance, immediately after Elida's passing, exactly what to write on the obituary form the newspaper had sent. Under "survived by" he had printed his name, and after it "husband." Then he'd added: "one daughter, Elmi, of Kansas City." He'd paused over the word "daughter" to consider "foster daughter," but finally had written "daughter." He hoped one of the relatives would send Elmi a copy. He was certain someone would.

This morning he had gone to the bedroom window again, as if he might find his wife walking to the crest of the hill as she had on that morning not long after Elmi had been taken. It was nearing the end of winter now, as it had been then, only during the night snow had fallen.

He dressed and walked out into the orchard. The cupped branches of the fruit trees seemed unnaturally bright, as if the whiteness of the snow caused them to vibrate in the sunlight.

One low branch of a plum tree under which he stood seemed laden with white blossoms. But when he reached for it, snow sloughed onto his jacket sleeve along the crook of his arm. He didn't shake it off, but began to walk with it, as if an invisible bird had landed on his arm and he wanted to carry it a few steps before it flew. When he finally let his arm drop, he felt a lightness ripple through his body, then lift away.

Widows were often given the job of tavern keeper, possibly to save their community the expense of looking after them. Probity and a reputation of chastity were essential for such a lady to obtain a license to "entertain travelers in the absence of relatives."

Coming

and

Going

The man at her door was bald and wore a blue windbreaker. She had asked him twice what he wanted, but he only said, "Are you Emily Fletcher?" as if he knew she was, but needed confirmation.

It struck her from the man's salutary tone that she might have won something—an envelope was about to be handed over with a check inside for a million dollars. She was sixty-five years old. It was about time.

"Yes," she said, her tone cascading downward, as if she were stepping onto an unsteady footbridge over a high mountain pass. The man looked harmless enough, there in the doorway. On closer observation he seemed less sure of himself, as if he couldn't quite fathom why he was there. So many things had seemed unfathomable to

Emily since her husband's recent death that she'd begun to accept "unfathomable" as an ongoing state.

Emily suddenly remembered she'd left Hanson, her lawyer, waiting on the telephone. It had taken her three phone calls to get a return call from him and now the dollars were ticking away while she stood there with this awkward stranger. She looked him over again and felt the moment seize her in which women hurriedly judge a man safe with the scantest evidence—that split second in which they lunge past fears into an unreliable security.

"Please step inside," Emily said. "I won't be a minute." She moved back to allow the man into the entry, then shut the door behind him and automatically turned the deadbolt. She knew it was crazy, to lock people in after she'd locked them out, but at least no one else would come in. She'd been interrupted by the telephone as she'd been taking a quilt from its shipping package. She had draped the gift from her sister across the back of a hall chair. She left the man standing as if he'd come to a halt before the flag of some unknown nation.

Speaking again to Hanson, she experienced the odd sensation of being two places at once. She heard her voice going out over the phone lines, but she was also uneasily aware that her side of the conversation was entering the acutely attentive but uncommunicative head of the stranger in her entryway.

"Nyal spent a month in Italy while the house was under construction, but it wasn't a vacation!" she said to Hanson. "Martin tells me this woman called him before his father died." She revealed this almost involuntarily. Martin was their son and she had confided unnecessarily to the lawyer during their last discussion that she feared Martin was a womanizer. She hated how she found herself blurting the most personal things to the business people she dealt with now. "It was while Nyal was very ill, and the woman must have intended to put pressure on him by calling Martin." She paused here to calculate the echo factor of the stranger's overhearing this last piece of information. Though what did it really matter? The man had no context in which to place these fragments of her life. Hanson's incisive voice, heading for the crux of the matter, began impatiently sweeping aside what he seemed to consider mere female baggage.

"The legal issue is: Did your husband modify, use, or appropriate another man's house design? And if so, is that man's widow entitled to recompense? The statute of limitations unfortunately has not run out on this. You're further involved because Nyal completed this job under the business partnership you both formed to reduce his tax liability. You signed off on this work and took payment with him in the partnership."

"I recall something about it," Emily said. "But Nyal took care of all that." She'd signed whatever Nyal had asked her to sign. At the time they'd formed the partnership, paper had flown by with blizzard force. But, as representative of her husband's estate and also in her tutelary capacity as his surviving business partner, she would now, Hanson had reminded her, be the defendant in any action. The other woman, also a widow, and representing her own deceased husband's estate in Rome, would be the plaintiff. On his behalf, she claimed part ownership in a house design. Nyal had only been asked to modify the design. The plans had resulted in a construction in Italy which Emily had never seen, but which her husband had supervised. Both men who'd contributed to its design were now dead—her husband from cancer and the architect named Riccardo from a stroke in Rome some ten months previously.

During the final months of her own husband's illness, Emily had been aware of murmurings from the widow in Rome, who believed Nyal owed her payment for Riccardo's original design. Ultimately a letter had arrived full of allegations. And Nyal, on his sickbed, had reasserted it was nonsense. Riccardo himself had invited him to modify the plan. Riccardo's widow knew this all very well. It was unfortunate Riccardo wasn't alive to corroborate it. But the whole matter would subside on its own. No, they needn't hire a lawyer in Rome.

For a time, Nyal seemed to have been right. They'd had their hands full, with people coming to visit and pay their respects, once it became known that Nyal's cancer was no longer in remission. Also, there was the finishing work on plans for the ecological center. Nyal had been the lead architect, and this project had been his final passion. All else had been swept aside so he could concentrate his remaining energies. The strange Italian murmuring had become inaudible, all but forgotten. Now Hanson informed her that yet another letter had arrived, one which framed the complaint so aggressively he suspected it was preliminary to a suit.

"We may need to get representation in Rome for the estate and for you as well, if she decides to press the matter," Hanson said. Emily tried to gauge the emphasis he was putting on the "if." Why was her lawyer so lackluster, such a practitioner of the uninflected? She could never tell where the meaning lay in his sentences. Since her husband's death she craved emotion in all her communications. This lawyer was an ongoing disappointment in this regard.

"Rome?" she heard herself saying, like a word spoken aloud in a dream. It was as well to say Djakarta or Bandar Seri Begawan. The only personal connection she'd had with Rome, other than her late husband's sojourn there, was having avoided the city while she'd traveled alone as a young woman in Europe. She had pointedly not gone to Italy when she'd heard that Italian men randomly and impulsively pinched women.

"Do you think I'll have to go to Rome?"

"It's possible," Hanson said. "But worse things have happened than a trip to Rome." Emily took note of a sound in the entryway and remembered the unknown man who, by now, must certainly have become restive. He might be deciding to go without having handed over the important, long-awaited envelope. She still behaved as if Nyal were in the house. Had he been there during the time prior to his illness, he would have heard the man at the door and come down. A mere two weeks had passed since his death and the house seemed swollen and randomly eruptive. At times it pulsed with an absence that was a kind of presence, a hum of consciousness that ran parallel to her own movements in the rooms.

"I'm glad Nyal didn't have to bear this," she found herself saying to Hanson, as if Nyal could still somehow overhear. But what she really meant was that she was sorry she was having to bear it alone. "I have to go. There's someone here," she said, allowing a provocative edge to slip into her voice. They agreed to speak later. She paused a moment before hanging up, hoping Hanson would give a small reassurance that this trouble was likely to subside, but he gave none.

She hung up feeling betrayed by things beyond her control, as if some still trembling fiber of her dead husband's actions had brought them into an unfamiliar alliance. Why had he taken on the project of a house in a foreign country? This Riccardo—someone he'd known from his college days who'd married and settled in Italy—

he'd involved Nyal, brought him in to solve an impasse on the project he'd begun. She only vaguely recalled. Nyal's expertise in the particular building materials had been important. But also something to do with an inflexible situation. Now some inflexible element had acquired another impetus. It was hardly conceivable that this had gotten so out of hand.

When she returned to the entry she found the casually dressed, rather timorous man examining the quilt. Black arrowhead-like sets of Vs dovetailed down the white fabric. There was something almost cruel about the pattern, but she identified with its pain-in-flight quality.

"It's the Widow's Quilt, a nineteenth-century pattern," she said to the man. "But in the quilt books the formal name is The Darts of Death."

"A lot of work there," the man said quietly, raising his eyes to her with what seemed a sepulchral gaze. He let the quilt edge slip from his fingers.

"I don't know quite where to use it. It's single-bed size." She felt at once she'd volunteered too much in speaking of a bed to a man she didn't know. She noticed him pull nervously on his jacket zipper, running it a short way down, then up toward his Adam's apple. There was a wedding ring on the hand. She felt herself drop her guard another notch.

"I have something to give you," the man said. The insupportable idea of the prize envelope fluttered tantalizingly again through Emily's mind. If it were to happen, it was a pity Nyal would miss it, she thought, characteristically undercutting anticipation with disappointment. The man definitively unzipped the jacket and reached inside to his shirt breast pocket. Next he extended a black leather holder the size of a checkbook and flipped it open to reveal a gold star on a dark velvet backing. It was a badge. It seemed the man was some sort of official.

"I'm a United States deputy marshal," he said, expertly returning the badge to his breast pocket. "And since you are Emily Fletcher, I have papers to leave with you. You'll need to sign, just to acknowledge you received them." He reached farther inside his jacket and brought forth a sheaf of official documents and handed them to her. She could see that everything, except the receipt form, was in another language.

"If you'd just sign here, please, Mrs. Fletcher," the man said without the slightest doubt in his manner that she would comply. He now had the air of someone for whom these matters were beneath notice. He produced a black pen and handed it to her. She followed his index finger to a signature line, under which she saw her name typed. She was still quaking from having glimpsed the gold star. What exactly was a deputy marshal? She felt unable to speak the question aloud. To ask could invite a revelation as to the seriousness of the matter. Was she about to be arrested? She wanted to flee her own house.

She folded back the signature page and quickly scanned the document for clues. It was in Italian, she confirmed from the legal address in Rome. Here, then, were the very documents her lawyer had feared were on the way. The word "press" came back from Hanson's characterization of what the aggrieved woman might do. She might *press* on with things." A sexual verb, Emily thought. So here the woman was, indeed. Pressing on. It struck her oddly that the coincidence of her lawyer's warning had merged into the arrival of the process server. It carried an eerie resonance, as if something awful were masquerading as normal, a thought she had experienced most poignantly at the moment of Nyal's death, the way his breath, in its final rush, had been so like a sigh.

Martin had said that when the woman telephoned three weeks ago, she'd claimed Nyal had once given her the number "in case I ever needed to reach your father." She'd informed Martin she would soon be taking the "necessary steps." Evidently it had not deterred the woman to learn from Martin that Nyal was terminally ill. Only after Nyal's death had Martin told Emily about having received this puzzling call. Maybe the woman, even now, believed and intended that her letters, followed by the serving of papers, would catch Nyal on the brink of his death. What sort of woman would do such a thing? She never wanted to become such a woman.

Emily held the papers and stared at her own name— again, the feeling of forces conjoining, of her consciousness swarmed with unsought intensity. She wanted to be rid of this man as quickly as possible. She moved her hand through the deft strokes with which she traversed her signature. During the days since her husband's death, she and their son had only once again referred to the woman in Italy.

"She can claim anything she likes, now that your father's dead," Emily had said. "She could claim they'd had an affair and that he promised her the moon!" The remark had flown out of her and she'd reveled briefly in the absurdity of its fictional self-inflicted wound, or perhaps the wound had been meant indirectly for Martin. "To call you—she seems desperate," Emily said. Her son dismissed the woman as the sort of person who's delusional, who has nothing fruitful to do with her life, so she runs around trying to extort money and to get attention by threatening to sue. He'd met this type, he said, in his job as an insurance adjuster. Martin was forty-three, had a darling third wife and five children from his two previous marriages. He loved to evaluate propositions, buildings, objects, and the erotic parameters of any female with whom he came into contact. Emily knew all this without surrendering affection for him. The more untrue he'd been to his wives, the more attentive and solicitous he had tended to be toward her. It consoled her now that he seemed to give no credence to this woman's claims.

"I'm sorry," the bald man said, lifting the stapled pages to yet another signature page. "Just here on the duplicate, if you'd be so good." He pointed to a red X near a blank. Emily wasn't at all sure she should be signing for these papers, but doing so was strangely as simple as the fact that the pen was in her hand. She signed again, then, without replacing the cap, handed the pen back to the man. His hands, like her own, were trembling. He was also finding the encounter stressful.

"Now," he said, and glanced pointedly toward the living room. "Could you tell me, please, is Mr. Fletcher here?" He paused and looked in the opposite direction, toward the kitchen. "Or has he relocated?" This second question startled her in the possibilities it opened up. She thought of the woman's audacity in having telephoned her son, the invasiveness of her having insinuated a dispute into such a time, when her husband's life had been reaching its final days and hours. And now this woman, who should have known what it was to suffer such a loss with her own husband not dead a year, had propelled a process server into her entry. There had obviously been some delay in the arrival of the papers, which must have been in the works prior to Nyal's death. The U.S. deputy marshal probably did not read Italian and had no idea what this was about. He was restless and only half satisfied in his accomplishment. He tucked the signed receipts inside his jacket, allowing Emily to retain the sheaf of paper in Italian. Then he regarded her as if she were withholding something. He seemed precariously on the verge of becoming less courteous. A set of undelivered papers still remained in his hands.

Emily's mind was speeding through the town. She could picture exactly where her husband lay—the freshly disturbed plot which overlooked the town at its eastern edge. There was a large evergreen wreath at the head of his grave, with NYAL and BELOVED HUSBAND AND FATHER in gold lettering on wide strands of velvet ribbon. It would be months before she arranged for the stone and decided what to inscribe on it, but there was a poem she already had in mind. It was a tanka by the Japanese poet Bashō— whose poem was modeled on yet another poem sent by a woman to a man after their first love-meeting. She might use only the first three lines:

> Was it you who came
> Or was it I who went—
> I do not remember.

She approved of the casualness of these lines, how they held a definitive absence in suspension, as some mere coming or going. The words would have yet another dimension, she realized, when her own remains eventually entered the plot beside her husband. It would be as if a conversation were still ongoing between them. Even while the poem subtracted their "remembering," it would insist on memory all the more for anyone who paused before the stone. But most of all, she agreed with how the words cast away life and death at one fell swoop.

There was something at once simple and expansive in that motion.

"Yes, my husband *has* relocated," she said, bringing her attention back to the man. It occurred to her that although she had no control over the serving of these papers, she did hold sway over the exact moment in which she stood.

"Would you be so kind as to tell me where I might find Mr. Fletcher," the bald man said.

"Certainly." Emily spoke clearly and decisively. "I'd be glad to help you find my husband." The man was clearly taken aback by her cooperativeness, as if he'd expected to be rudely dismissed. He shifted the remaining papers to his right hand and ran the hand with the wedding ring over the top of his pale head and let it drop. He then shifted his feet in a maneuver that brought him backward and into contact with the Widow's Quilt. His demeanor, she saw, had visibly softened when she said she would help. It was likely he'd experienced harsh treatment many times. He did not smile, but dropped his shoulders, which had been held high and rather formally.

"There's a very nice view of the town where my husband has landed," Emily said. She disliked the casual implication of "landed," since she and Martin had carefully chosen the site. Nonetheless, she was determined to continue in this fashion, to reveal exactly where her husband was.

"Oh, very good," the man said. He resituated the sheaf of documents meant for her husband inside his jacket, then plunged a hand into his trouser pocket, jingling some loose change, no doubt an unconscious expression of delight at the surrender he assumed on her part.

"Go east on First, past the bowling alley, and down

Race until you come to Caroline," she directed. The man took a small notebook from a side jacket pocket and began to scribble. "Then turn right and continue past the hospital. You'll approach some grassy fields, then go up a steep hill. At the top you'll find the development you're looking for." To call a graveyard a "development" would never have occurred to her, but she supposed death was a development. Still, her husband's death was beyond the word in such a physically challenging way that she felt an involuntary shiver run through her.

"I imagine there's a house number," the man said.

"If you need assistance to find exactly where Mr. Fletcher's situated," Emily said, "ask at the little white house just inside the gate. There's someone on duty until five P.M."

Emily thought she'd deflected the reference concerning the house number nicely. The man glanced at his watch and Emily automatically checked her own. She saw that only half an hour remained for the man to get further help in finding her husband. He slipped the notebook with the instructions back into his side pocket.

"You've been most cooperative," he said, and glanced uncomprehendingly at the ferocious black darts of the Widow's Quilt which, as he brushed against it, seemed to be jutting directly into him. For a moment she thought crazily that, in his mute exuberance, he intended to embrace her. The idea made her quake, as when he'd flashed his deputy marshal's badge. She was relieved when he reached for the door handle and attempted to let himself out. She moved near his shoulder, turned the deadbolt and moved back so he could pass. On the steps he paused, turned toward her and uttered some final sentence of courtesy, then crossed the driveway to his white Volvo. She was taking pleasure in the very fact of his going and that he would now be following her directions, this minion of the widow in Rome. He climbed into his car, then lifted his hand in a mild wave. She did not return the gesture.

She was thinking of her husband now, that he could not know these unpleasant things which had befallen her since his death, strangers who wanted to use his silence to beleaguer and ensnare her. Nyal would have enjoyed how she'd just acquitted herself. She imagined the two of them laughing about the U.S. deputy marshal's driving into the cemetery, hoping to be directed out of a wrong turn, asking the caretaker where Nyal Fletcher "lived." Well, the widow in Rome had misused Emily's husband, and now Emily would make use of her messenger. The man could stand before her husband's wreath as long as he wanted. Maybe Emily's circumstances would prick his heart. He might fully experience the weight of his actions that day. After all, they had each been reduced to functionaries.

She continued to follow the man in her mind as she gathered the quilt so the darts folded against her breasts and grazed her neck. She carried it upstairs to the queen-size bed she now occupied alone. She spread the quilt out on her side. With the pattern unfurled, the bed seemed to be sliced in two, but the quilt gave her side fresh vitality. Even though it was hours before bedtime, she unbuttoned her dress, stepped out, then lifted the covers and crawled between the sheets in her slip. The added weight was an unexpected comfort. She closed her eyes, then eased her hand onto her husband's side of the bed. It was cooler and she realized that her cheeks, against the white pillowcase, were flushed.

She thought of the woman in Rome. What if? she thought, and Emily smiled to recall the moment with

Martin in which she had cast her dead husband into the woman's arms in a sentence uttered more as a challenge to the unlikely than a true possibility. But what would it change if her husband had sought the company of another woman? How casually the thought came to her. They had been married the same forty-five years. She believed they had loved each other beyond all others. She even recalled the exact site of her faith, her steadfast belief. One night, before they were to go out in company, he'd put his arms around her at the door and said, "If I should ever say anything to annoy you while we're out, dear, ignore it, because I adore the ground you walk on." It was gallant and wide, and no one had said anything so beautiful to her before or since.

Death had added another dimension to that long-ago gift. Perhaps it was death, that ultimate release from belonging, which made even the idea of infidelity ludicrous. She suddenly caught a glimpse of a possibility she'd kept quietly in reserve. She wondered if all wives held aside a reserve of forgiveness for unrevealed betrayals, believing their husbands could, in some pull of opportunity, go astray in fact, if not in heart? She had put aside such a reserve, she saw, without really having had to know it, until now. Yet: *so what?*

Prior to the Italian woman's intrusion which had forced her to tremble in her own doorway, she'd had no idea of the degree to which she could still volunteer acceptance of all Nyal might have been. It was really in behalf of them both that she could manage this leap. At his death she had thought mistakenly that an end had come to the growth of their earthly loving, but instead she had stepped onto unexpected terrain where what she held precious had become even more so. In these thoughts she was able to reach herself newly, and this both surprised and enlarged her sense of Nyal and of their life together. In her heart's reception of all her husband might have experienced, in and out of her knowledge, she saw with an ungaugeable onrushing force how deeply she'd loved him and loved him still. Would always love him.

"You're so very kind," the U.S. deputy marshal had said to her as he'd gone down the porch steps. Her throat tightened now as she recalled his words. She had not been at all kind toward this man, and by now he would be realizing this. What was there in being kind when life itself and the actions of others were often monstrous? Yet she continued to believe kindness was, when one could manage it, the ultimate checkmate, and beyond that, the one enviable gift. But could there be a hidden sleeve of malice inside too much kindness? Whatever else, she'd been true to her feeling.

Nyal's silence seemed more vast than ever, and she felt included there—allowing all things to be absorbed, to coexist—fidelity and infidelity, residence and grave, coming and going.

By now the man had likely reached his destination. He would have come to stand before the wreath. For a moment he might have studied the name on the fluttering ribbon. Then, deciding to go, he would have turned and begun to walk back to his car. Perhaps he was ruefully thinking of her this very moment, of how artfully she'd misled him. But maybe, if he hadn't passed too far into disgruntlement, he might pause and look back toward the grave, realizing that, on either side of the town, they could both be faintly smiling.

My Lulu, she's a dandy,
She stands and drinks like a man,
She calls for gin and brandy,
And she doesn't give a damn,
And she doesn't give a damn.

Madame Mustache—"She knew how to defend herself."

My

Gun

I am thirty-eight, have straight teeth and good hygiene. When anyone from the thin-is-godly camp looks me over like I should lose a pound or two, I tell them, "Sorry. I protect my roundness." Although I haven't yet tried to write a personals ad to attract somebody new, I think once I figured out the codes, I could come up with something punchy and tantalizing. Now that a year has passed since my husband's death, I start to think about such things.

Lately, however, the question of whether or not I should buy my own gun seems to preoccupy me more than whether I should look for a new mate. I ask you, what kind of country is it where a woman finds herself considering a gun for a companion? When my husband was alive, the idea of owning and using a gun never occurred to me. I'm not even sure at this point why I feel myself inching toward the moment I'm actually forking over cash for a little snub-nosed silver something, dropping it into my purse, and walking out of this one particular gun shop I've had my eye on, just east of town.

This shop attracts me because it sprang up overnight like a bad mushroom. It looks as if it could be staffed by the same men—why am I certain they are men?—selling arms elsewhere in the world—to Bosnian Serbs, or helping the Macedonians get ready in case their towns are next, or beefing up Croatian arsenals. Just the thought of those Serbs, according to belated reports from national observers, raping several thousand women for three years as an actual so-called "weapon of war"—now this makes me want to rush right out and buy my gun.

It scares me when I think like this. But then, many things come to my mind, now that I'm alone. I have too much time to think, according to my friends. Most of the time I wouldn't even say I am "thinking." I muse a lot. I especially like to muse in my flower garden which borders the property my husband and I kept as a summer home, but to which I have now retreated full-time. When I'm musing I dislike being interrupted. My neighbor, who's about fifty and who practically lives in her yard, is always trying to carry on conversations with me.

"We have twenty-one cats in our neighborhood," she says. "I didn't count yours since he never comes outside. These are outdoor cats I'm talking about."

My neighbor is fuming on the cat question because *someone* has dropped a flyer into her mailbox. It suggests that those who have outdoor cats keep them indoors during the entire spring and early summer months, because birds are nesting and raising their young.

"Cats have to do their cat things," she says. "Why should I confine mine when twenty other cats are on the prowl?"

At precisely 8 A.M. every morning my neighbor scatters a stingy handful of seed on a hip-high platform in her backyard. I have never pointed out to her that these feeders are patently death traps for birds. In neighborly tolerance I allow her to bait, entrap, and tantalize to her heart's content.

Aside from cats and birds, my neighbor can be nosy in other ways. Like asking if the investigation is still going on as to why my husband, a well-known progressive senator from a southern state, committed suicide. I correct her right away.

"Not suicide. Nobody knows. But not suicide."

"I'm sorry," she says, and I believe she is, in her own way, sorry. "I only know what I read in the papers," she says, deftly hinting.

"I can't really talk about it," I say, though I'd like to. But I don't want to ruin the nest of my musing. How would it be if, every time I stepped into the yard to water my sweet peas, my neighbor and I had to talk about my husband's death?

One thing I know: my husband was a man who loved every instant of life, and no way did he shoot himself in the back of the head at that impossible angle. For one thing, he had a muscle problem in his right shoulder. He had dislocated it a number of times during the three years we were married. I used to rub liniment on that shoulder every night.

Of course, it's true, I didn't know he kept a handgun that was registered to him with his own apparent signature. If he could keep a handgun secret from me, he could also conceivably intend suicide and not give hints. No matter what anyone says, I think suicide is totally out of character for him.

From her remarks in the press, his ex-wife seemed to accept the idea of his suicide a bit eagerly, I thought. At the funeral I wanted to ask her a few things, but I never got a chance. She made an awful racket at the graveside and had to be kept from leaping onto my husband's coffin. It was probably a mistake even to think we could have spoken peaceably to each other, since even now she considers herself the "authentic widow," essentially because she put in more time with my husband.

My husband was an obsessive preparer. This may have caused me not to notice things I should have. I don't know if he had this habit of preparing for the worst during what he referred to as his "interminable marriage" to his first wife. Right from the time we were married he frequently used the phrase "If anything happens to me . . ." He was twenty years older and he knew it was likely I would survive him.

"Here's my safe-deposit key," my husband had said. "Notice the shape and color. Your other keys look silver, but this one's tarnished, clouded like pewter." He slipped it onto my key ring, right next to my rabbit's foot. "If anything happens to me, look in the safe-deposit box."

My husband believed in safety nets and he told me from the start he had insurance to cover payments on both our houses, the one on the East Coast and the one where I now live, the location about which I can't be specific. Naturally the suicide question put a kink in his preparations, and I am on the verge of losing both houses. Soon I may have no garden in which to muse, no well-meaning neighbor to avoid.

"You should get yourself a gun and let me teach you how to use it," my neighbor is saying, as I douse my sweet peas with Miracle Grow. "Bruce and I worry about you," she says, "over there by yourself in that big house." She doesn't say *alone*. And *woman* is the other word we take for granted.

"I know how to shoot. I'm also a crack shot," my neighbor says. "I could snap off the nose of a reindeer at two hundred yards." It's when she says things like this that I realize I wouldn't trade this neighbor for anyone on the planet. She is better than a security system or a pack of pit bull terriers. Plus, she makes me laugh, which is curative.

I'm aware that she practices her marksmanship because on Sundays I see her blue Ford station wagon parked just off the highway in front of the shooting range. She goes to church, then comes home, grabs her gun and drives over to the range to shatter clay pigeons for an hour or two. Sometimes Bruce goes with her. Maybe she and my husband shattered clay pigeons elbow to elbow, but I don't ask.

When I'm unresponsive she says, "If you need me, I'm just a phone call away." She is a good and thoughtful neighbor, it's easy to see, and I believe she would bring her loaded gun over here in the early morning hours and shoot to kill if she found me in any possible danger. And Bruce, he would be right behind her with his gun. I would have a small but capable army of two at my disposal. These are people whose consciences would not wince, or be hampered in the least, by slamming a bullet through somebody's heart or brain if they found such a person climbing through one of my windows or breaking down a door. "Hesitate and ye are lost" is their motto, and "Let the police ask questions of their relations later." When I muse about getting a gun I often think I should instead put a sign at the entrance to my property which says: Beware: Neighbors Armed & Dangerous. Then I wouldn't have to continue this dialogue with myself about the advisability of owning a gun.

It's funny how just beginning to consider getting a gun feeds all sorts of personal encounters into the question. Last week a girlfriend in an upscale area of San Francisco calls me, shaken to the core. She has zapped open her garage door and gone inside, only to find a man behind her. Two seconds later he puts a knife to her throat. She is dressed in a pretty summer smock with a dropped neckline and carrying a purse, just for looks, with no more than twenty dollars cash in it. My mother would say my friend has brought this on herself by dressing this way. Whatever. My friend is under attack and coming up short. Her credit cards—she can see them now—are zippered into her regular purse in the downstairs closet. Listening to her is like watching a reenactment on a TV cop show.

"The guy is pissed because I'm an empty cash register," my friend says. "Then he spots my wedding ring. He orders me to take it off. It's my great-grandmother's ring and just to think of this worse-than-scum taking it is like throwing generations down a sewer. But I can't get it off my finger.

" 'Let up on my neck,' I breathe to the creep through my teeth. 'Maybe I can suck it loose.'

" 'Get it off, bitch, or you're blood on cement,' the guy says.

"I can't see the man's face because he's behind me, but I am ashamed to be glad the arm around my neck is a white arm. Honey, why, as a white woman in America, have I been caused, against my will, to think, *Hey, shouldn't this guy mugging me be black?* Where did this designer thought come from, and why do I suspect I'm not alone in having it?" my friend asks.

I'm used to her rants and can generally cut through the haze to touch down on the other side. I admit I'm more concerned about her throat getting sliced than her political and sociological quandaries. But then, just having a throat to be cut, like having a gun to fire—these are new concerns for me. And white arm, black arm—if the throat is cut, it bleeds.

"So I'm sucking away on my ring," she says, "and the white arm has let up enough that I could get my whole hand into my mouth if my mouth was big enough. Finally the ring clinks against my teeth, and rolls to the back of my tongue so I nearly swallow it. I have to bend into the knife to keep the ring out of my throat. I manage to spit it onto the garage floor, and he shoves me to the cement where I get a mechanic's view of my car. This is life in America.

"I am still afraid he's going to bend over and slit me open like a melon," she says. "But the white arm reaches behind one of the car tires and grabs my ring. Next, I see these big feet in high-powered Nikes loping off into the daylight. I reach up and touch my throat. There is blood on my fingers when I bring them away. I pull myself up and tremble back inside the house to a mirror. There's a hairline slice where I had to bend into the knife. I call the police and then I phone Bobby, who's so furious I won't even repeat what he said, and who assumes I've been raped. And hey, there is that black guy again. The one who wasn't there. 'Was the guy black?' That's the first thing Bobby wants to know. Not: 'How are you, babe? Are you all right?' "

Bobby is my friend's husband and it turns out he owns a gun. He's been trying to convince my friend she should get one too. By the time of this conversation, she has been to her first gun-handling session. She has her mind around a trigger and is saying, "I never thought I'd be so totally *into* anything like this, but I am. Our instructor put it to us like this: 'Would you rather be carried by six or judged by twelve?' "

"And do you feel safer?" I ask, dreading the answer.

"You bet holes in your panty hose," she said. "I'm not to be messed with." She went on to say that just having the gun in her possession made her more aware of danger. "I will never go into my garage again without my hand in my bag on my loaded gun." She had bought a special purse, she said, with a Velcro side pocket made just for her gun. She won't even have to take it out of the compartment to fire it. Just pull the Velcro tab, and BLAM!

It all sounded eerily reasonable, given what she'd been through. The hairline slice on her throat lingered in my mind when I walked into my own garage after that, and I thought of my gun out there somewhere, waiting for me to buy it and carry it everywhere like a mother kangaroo. I felt a glint of unattached affection for it spike off me into the cosmos.

I have begun to think a revolver would be my weapon of choice. I just like the word "revolver," though the word "automatic" also has its charm. If I were buying a new microwave I would go into the store and look at them. Run my hands over them. Open and shut them. See what buttons there were to push and how big the cook space is. Muffins versus turkey—that sort of thing. But going into a gun shop—the idea strikes me the same way going into a porn shop might. I feel all scummy and wrong just thinking about it. Like something I don't agree with is going to happen.

But then, I'm a widow and this is also something to which I didn't agree. I think of him all the time, my husband, out there under the dirt where I know he doesn't want to be.

Not long after his funeral I'm back to doing just what he told me. I take the deposit-box key down to the bank and have the girl let me into a room that is positively chilly with money. We each insert keys. I turn mine, then she slides out a long metal box. I carry it to a little alcove and sit down. For a moment I think of my husband, that he intended for me to do this. It's a bustling place, this bank, but my alcove is a still pool of silence. The sort of silence I imagine around my husband when he was shot. Or, if I'm wrong, the silence he broke when he shot himself.

I lift the lid. Inside are my husband's will and the papers on our houses. But in a long brown envelope I discover several thick bundles of traveler's checks. One-thousand-dollar checks, unsigned. Packets and packets of checks. Why did my husband put so much money in here, money which was never invested and also has not been collecting one cent of interest? Where has this money come from? Did we pay taxes on it? Should I report it to someone? I mean, this is more money than I have ever seen before in my life. I am not even going to mention the total amount.

My mother's descriptions of hot flashes come back to me because I am sweating right through my favorite apple-print top. The traveler's checks seem tainted, cut off from the whole idea of spending. It's true I could use them, even bail myself out of my current financial problem caused by my husband's assumed suicide. I could pay off the mortgage on one of the houses, probably the one next door to my armed-and-dangerous neighbors. "If anything ever happens to me," I recall my husband saying. But what did he intend with this stash of ready-to-travel money? Am I supposed to go someplace, and if so, where?

I hate the paralysis of this decision period I'm in. I phone a woman I met at a fund-raiser for my husband's last campaign. She's a performance artist living in L.A. When she started telling ex-wife stories at the party, we hit it off right away. We even joked about doing a book together called *The Men We Love and the Bitches They Left.* Our plan would be to write this under aliases, so as not to get sued by our respective ex-wife antagonists.

"What about guns?" I ask her. "Do you own one?"

"No," she says. "But I've handled one. I went over to this guy's, Stan Mosman—Mossy, we call him. He has guns all over his apartment, the way some people collect masks or ships in bottles. I tell him, 'I want to do a performance piece in which I load a real gun with real bullets, then point it at my audience while I do my monologue—some ramble about having gone off my meds because I was losing my edge.' This appeals to him. 'How can I help you?' he asks. I tell him I need to learn to handle a gun so it's second nature. He takes a handgun out of a locked cabinet and slides it onto the coffee table in front of me with a shivery metal-on-wood *thunk.* When I pick it up, it's heavier than I expected, but more than that—the power, the diabolical nature of the thing. No doubt about it, I've got my hand around pure evil, something made to kill people. My whole body is horrified. After a few moments I just ease it back onto the table and say, 'Mossy—thanks a lot, but I'm going to have to borrow a gun from props. A real gun is just a little *too* real.' "

Listening to my actress friend's experience is like being an astronaut of my gun question. I begin to see all sides of it. The way she'd felt about the gun is close to how I'd felt about the checks in the lockbox. Something unsavory. Too many unknowns. Then my friend begins to describe her neighborhood and I realize she has more reason than I do to start down this should-I-get-a-gun path.

"So I walk back from Mossy's to my apartment," my friend continues. "Remember, I live in the Echo Park area of L.A. Still, it's weird to see black spray-painted messages that say RIP SPOOKY on telephone poles and the sides of buildings." She assumes I know what this means. When I ask, she translates: "Rest In Peace, Spooky."

"Spooky," she says, "was a kid not six blocks from me who was shot to death in a gang showdown." It gives me a jolt of confidence to know that my friend, in such an environment, has chosen *against* owning a gun. But then she's an actress and could probably fake her way out of anything. She would just bite the white arm, and if the guy caught up to her, she'd offer first aid so convincingly he'd forget whatever he meant to do to her.

Recently I've tried to shift the focus of my musings from guns to a certain man who attracted my attention at a party after a production of *My Fair Lady*. He is physically impressive, looks able to lift and move things—more and more this is how I judge the desirability of a man. I noticed immediately that he would be fit enough to help reorganize the boxes I've stored in my garage—my husband's things, which I've kept for a museum. This man talked about how he loved to hike in the backcountry and, before I left, gave me his phone number on a scrap of paper he tore from a newspaper. He said he had a van that he often used as a camper. This added information seemed a little forward and suggestive, but I ignored it.

Even though my husband is gone, I still have friends in helpful places. One of them has access to records at the county courthouse. She offered to check out this gentle-man. A day later she calls in a great state of alarm. She has not only checked the courthouse files, but has asked around at her hairdresser's and the tanning salon.

"This guy's a real zero," she says. "Less than zero, if you want to know. Besides that, he has a permit to carry a gun. Trouble," she says. "If I were you, I'd just crumple that phone number and toss it into the nearest public toilet."

But I don't do anything of the sort. I put the number into my coat pocket and head for the supermarket. It's a ten-minute drive through the usual heavy afternoon traf-fic. I go inside and locate the magazine racks. At least ten different gun magazines are available. I decide on one with a photograph of a woman, arms extended, both hands grasping her handgun with the tension of a sling-shot, before the target of a shadow-man. There are already lethal holes in this "man."

It occurs to me that if this target were in the shape of a woman, with bullet holes arranged like erogenous zones, I wouldn't be buying this magazine. I notice I am willing, at least in my imagination, to shoot holes into the shape of a man. I wonder, could this be one of those designer thoughts my San Francisco friend was talking about?

The female cashier acts like I'm not doing anything special buying this magazine, but I've camouflaged it with necessities—milk and raisin bread. Maybe she's a gun owner herself. It's not something I'd know how to ask. As I walk to my car I think I see the attractive man getting into his van. I situate my groceries in the back seat, then reach into my coat pocket and touch the slip of newsprint on which our link is scribbled.

Back home, I carry in the groceries. I take my gun magazine into the bedroom and place it on the night-stand, saving it for bedtime. It's late afternoon, so I go outside and unspool the hose to do my watering. A fat white cat dodges into the shrubbery when he sees me. I assume he's had experiences.

I begin to muse about the attractive man as I water my sweet peas and glads, the hanging baskets and rosemary. Then I muse on the word "inevitable," whether my husband felt his death was, in any sense, inevitable when he loaded up the lockbox with traveler's checks for me to find. My neighbor fills her birdbath and we wave reassuringly to each other from the parameters of our yards.

Later I make a trip to town because I need to drop something at my lawyer's, the one still trying to unravel my husband's financial affairs. I drive past the gun shop, which is covered with fishnet and painted camouflage green and gray. The phone number of the attractive man with a gun permit is in my pocket. I wonder what make of gun he packs. Having his number is like having a gun, without having it. Just to know he's there, if I need him. Loaded and ready. I am certain he would teach me all I need to know about guns. I might even invent some trigger-happy love-name for him, like Spooky or Mossy, and we'd go off to shoot clay pigeons together on Sundays. Or maybe he lives in the country, where we could shatter the windshields of junked cars. The scrap of paper curls around my finger and causes a ripple to run up my spine, just to know he's there. Naturally, I don't plan to use his number. I hope that's clear.

"Oh my God," said Paula, "he isn't even wearing a tie!"

1. *Place the wide end of the tie on your right so it hangs about twelve inches longer than the narrow end.*
2. *Wrap the long end around the short end and then behind, finishing on the right.*
3. *Continue to cross long end over short end, finishing on the left.*
4. *Pull long end through loop from the back.*
5. *Slip point through front of knot and tighten.*
6. *While pulling down short end with one hand, use other hand to slide knot up snugly.*

Mr. Woodriff's
Neckties

Every now and then one of her visitors carries an item of clothing out to their car and hangs it with their own. Sometimes they're clutching a paper bag and I can't see what she has given away. Shirts and books, and even his toiletries, though I'm just guessing here. I'm probably mistaken about the toiletries. But things have been trickling out of the house ever since she began to get a grip on herself.

About a year ago she told me over the fence that she might not be able to keep her house. Legal matters, including Mr. Woodriff's royalties given over to pay off a publisher for books he'd never write. It's been a hard time for each of us in our own way.

Mr. Woodriff only managed to live ten months in the

house next door as my neighbor. I'm a good neighbor and I would have enjoyed living next to him into old age. Maybe even seeing myself depicted as a minor character, walking a dog or passing by just as his main character needed to clarify something by speaking with a stranger.

EVEN THOUGH our time as neighbors was short, I had some good influence on things next door. Mr. Woodriff used to ask me about my roses. I guess he could tell I'm a fanatic about them. He told me his literary agent in New York City had sent him and his wife three rose plants— Love, Hope, and Cherish. The next thing I knew he and his wife were making a small rose garden over there with about ten bushes. She would dig a hole with a mattock. Then she would haul a gallon bucket of water over next to the planting bed and he would tip the water into the hole, then wait for it to seep into the soil. Finally, he would get down on his knees and set each plant into place.

On Sundays I see her gathering these same roses, now that they've bloomed, to take to the cemetery. It makes me wonder if they both knew while they were planting them that this was out there in the future. Or maybe they were so involved with earth and root balls and whether the holes were deep enough that they didn't trouble to think ahead, except that eventually there would be roses. Maybe their minds were mercifully clear of the future. That's what I hope, anyway.

I own signed copies of all of Mr. Woodriff's books, except this last one he was writing next door to me and which didn't get published until after his death. I called out to him one day while he was sitting on the teak bench in his yard, musing. Even before I saw it, I could smell he was smoking one of those small, stinky cigars. I stood at the fence and asked if I could please get his signature on a few books.

I was afraid he might be working, puzzling over a character in his head. I hated to disturb him. I've tried my hand at writing and I know how it goes—courting the imagination, putting words down until a new world builds up, mixing a little of the real with some of the made-up until it starts things you couldn't expect. I also know I'm never so happy as when I am reading, and I had never imagined that a real and famous writer—in fact, a pair of them, since the missus is also a writer—would move in next door to me.

When I asked Mr. Woodriff to sign the books, he appeared almost boyish. He seemed eager to do it for me, so I climbed through the rail fence and went over to him. I think he was not supposed to be smoking, because he acted like I had caught him at something. He puffed a rancid swirl of smoke onto some red peonies at one end of the bench and ground the cigar into the grass with the heel of his bedroom slipper. I noticed his heel stayed on the cigar.

"Sit down, sit down," he said to me, because he could see it was going to be a while, as I had brought about six books over that first time. I sat down at the far end of the bench and put the stack of books between us, then handed him my pen.

My wife was still living at this time and Mr. Woodriff very kindly inquired after her. I said she was now in remission and we were hoping, God willing, she would stay that way. I felt a little emboldened by actually being in his yard. I told him I lit a candle for him at Mass every time I lit one for my wife. He didn't seem embarrassed at all about this. In fact, he just very quietly said, "Thank you." Maybe I should have let it go at that, but I added that I hoped his treatments were going okay. There was no use pretending I didn't know he was traveling back and forth every week for radiation.

"I'm doing just fine," he said. "Nothing to it. It's over in sixty seconds and I don't feel a thing."

Before they left for Seattle one day I'd asked if I could do anything to help out, and his wife allowed me to water her sweet peas, which are on a trellis up against my fence. That's when she'd told me about the brain radiation.

The brain—well, it gave me pause, I can tell you, to think what might be going through Mr. Woodriff's mind, and his wife's, too—knowing there was a tumor where he worked and imagined. Still, I learned later he was going to his desk over there every day, writing those last things, and she was helping him.

After my wife's death, when I finally came to myself again, I noticed my neighbor's yard needed mowing, and I asked her would she mind if I ran my mower over it. She said her brother had been mowing it while he'd been out of work, but he'd recently found a real job. She would have to hire somebody all right, she said.

I told the widow it was no trouble and it would give me pleasure to mow her lawn, as by now I had read her stories and poems, too, along with Mr. Woodriff's. I'd also read about their life together—the final portions of which I'd witnessed without quite knowing what I was seeing.

There was the day a stocky Mexican with a pretty blond woman and a dark-haired beauty of a girl, his wife and daughter, I assume, pulled up with an unwieldy flat object strapped to the top of their avocado-green station wagon. At the time I thought it was a piece of construction material and that maybe this fellow was doing Sheetrock over there.

Later, when I'd been invited into the house, I saw that what I'd thought was Sheetrock was actually an oil painting this Mexican had painted. The canvas had been wrapped for transport in a bedsheet. If it hadn't been for this, I would have seen salmon leaping up a waterfall and the faint images of spirit-fish headed the opposite direction in the painted sky—all of this bobbing down the driveway between the Mexican and the blonde and onto the porch next door.

I discovered about the painting the day Mr. Woodriff motioned to me and asked would I come into the house to help him with something. "Sure. You bet," I said, and followed him into the entryway under a chandelier tall as one of those thirty-gallon galvanized garbage cans.

I thought he was going to ask me to help him move something and I was already deciding not to say anything about my sciatic nerve—just to take a chance I'd be okay. But instead he opened the hall-closet door and took out a necktie. He left the door open and I couldn't help noticing there were a lot of ties looped over wire clothes hangers at one end of the closet. These neckties were already tied, as if around an invisible neck, and the neck holes had been left wide to let the guy breathe or at least relax.

Mr. Woodriff ushered me into the TV room, which was very comfortable. I saw he must be spending a lot of time reading. At one end of a leather couch which faced into the room was a stack of books on the floor. I appreciated that the natural light over the back of the couch was good for reading.

When I turned back to Mr. Woodriff, he was holding this slightly metallic-looking, pale, salmon-colored necktie. There was an expression of utter helplessness on his face, and the tie was limp across his outspread palms like a priest bearing the Eucharist. If we had been in church my chin would have been up, eyes closed, and my tongue slightly extended.

"Do you know how to tie one of these?" Mr. Woodriff asks me.

At first I'm taken aback—a grown man who doesn't know how to tie a necktie? Then I recall reading somewhere that his father carried a lunch bucket. So did mine, and he didn't own a tie for some years himself. Still, I had to wonder how Mr. Woodriff made it in the halls of academe back East when he occasionally held a lectureship or a chair at this or that Ivy League university, times he must have had to meet a dean or two, or to look snappy in his tweed jacket at a banquet. Who was tying his necktie then? Somebody, or several somebodies, had certainly stocked his closet with a good supply of ready-to-slip-on neckties.

I am a man who is always learning things, so I assumed that finally Mr. Woodriff had decided to transcend his working-class preference for an open collar. He was ready to tie his own necktie and I was to be his teacher. I felt very flattered by this. I almost wished his wife were there to witness the patience I was about to expend in showing her husband how to do something which, for unknown reasons, he'd been avoiding all his life. But I'd seen her leave half an hour earlier in the car with some book-sized packages I'd assumed were for the post office.

"It's a tie one of my friends gave me," Mr. Woodriff said, "and I want to wear it at the book fair in Anaheim."

"Fine," I said. "We'll fix you up." He stood looking at me with a kind of friendly curiosity while I draped the tie around my neck. It did not coordinate with the mostly red plaid flannel shirt I was wearing. I asked Mr. Woodriff to move parallel to me while I went through the steps. I flipped the tie this way and that, as slowly as possible.

Finally, when I'd asked several times, "You got that?" and repeated the procedure, I handed him the tie and told him to give it a shot. He looked baffled. Like I'd just asked him to nail his eyeball to the wall while holding the hammer between his teeth. He laughed nervously. His fingers seemed ribbed together like wings. Then he made his move. He fanned one end of the tie over the other with a nice emphatic gesture that allowed me to think briefly this would come out okay after all.

But then he just stood there, elbows out, and looked down at the tie, which was shooting off a cruel iridescent sheen in the mid-morning sunlight. I wanted to give him a hint, but I also didn't want to insult his intelligence, which was considerable, despite what I'm portraying here.

When Mr. Woodriff made the first wrong move I reached up and gently got him headed right again. Finally, though, he'd made enough wrong moves that I realized something. I'd done it. I'd tied the tie for him!

He seemed very pleased. Extraordinarily pleased. He shook my hand enthusiastically, I remember, just like I'd done something for him nobody else had ever done. But it was dawning on me that this must have happened many times before, and that Mr. Woodriff had no earthly intention, before death and God, of ever learning to tie a necktie. I mean, it was right over there on the side of his ledger with bungee jumping and ice fishing, with camel rides across the Australian desert, and maybe even the Pogo Stick Olympics.

"This is great! This will keep me going just fine!" he said, and walked a few steps away into the bathroom so he could check my work in the mirror. The collar on his sports shirt wasn't right for a tie, but I guess he was picturing himself in his dress shirt and suit jacket. He liked what he saw.

Then he did something I realized I'd seen in my mind's eye a moment before it happened. He reached up, and like a sheriff who has interrupted a small-town lynching, he loosened the tie from his throat and lifted it over his head.

My neighbor seemed suddenly more free, like any man who's nearly lost his life. How could I help but be glad for him? I knew what he was up against, in more ways than one. I forgot all about being his failed teacher-of-the-necktie. Instead I looked around the room at the warm spruce paneling, the braided rug, the way the sun, shining through the skylight, illuminated the very place he was standing. I just appreciated the comfortable circumstances Mr. Woodriff had managed to find for himself. I knew from things his wife had said over the fence that it was a difficult time for him.

"Look at this painting our friend Alfredo gave us," Mr. Woodriff said, as he pushed me eagerly along by my elbow toward the living room. But I stopped in the dining room doorway, staring into the living room at this huge painting. Salmon were leaping across it. I took in the way they were balancing there on the edges of their deaths. Some were in the river and others were leaping above a waterfall. I had to fight the impulse to touch the painting, to feel the ridges in the river current and the waterfall. Mr. Woodriff must have noticed my hands rising, hovering before the painting, because he said, "Go ahead. It's okay."

I looked to see if my hands were clean and they were. Then I moved them very lightly with the current, across the canvas. It felt like minnows flicking against my fingertips. Still, I knew nothing was really moving except the blood in my veins. I let my fingers follow the lines of color and shape the Mexican painter had spent a month or more pressing into this canvas with oil paint on a brush. It occurred to me that all the time he must have been painting he had to know his friend was dying. He would have had to guess that. Yet he'd also probably been glad Mr. and Mrs. Woodriff had each other—that had to strike him. And the fish too. He must have been glad, as he painted each one, that nothing was going to get in the way of their leaping along like that.

It was all there in that painting—joy and sadness and destiny and friendship and farewell. I admit I was weak in the knees when I turned back into the room. I saw Mr. Woodriff, my neighbor, still holding the necktie he was going to slip back over his head in a few days in California, cinching it up to his Adam's apple like he'd tied it himself.

I was his accomplice, and we smiled at each other that day in his living room, like we'd just cleaned out a bank and each of us had a pretty woman waiting for us to spend the money on her. And we did, too—both of our wives still with us then, and that miracle of life itself, too, ours—for however long it lasted. We had it all.

THAT WAS the most memorable encounter I had with Mr. Woodriff. When his son comes to stay a few days each summer with his stepmother, my widowed neighbor, I feel strangely like I'm back in Mr. Woodriff's young vigorous days, shaking hands with him at full strength, his hand pressing so hard on mine that the wedding ring I've moved onto my right hand smarts to the bone.

"So, you knew my dad," the son says to me in a kind of simple wonderment, smiling. He's the spitting image of his father, only young and alive.

"I did," I say. "I sure did." And I'm sorry I don't have more to add, since my meetings with his father were really so incidental. I suppose I could tell him about the neckties, but somehow I think that's just between Mr. Woodriff and me.

Sometimes I look over and see the son sitting alone where his father sat on the teak bench. I've noticed him helping my neighbor pick the apples when he occasionally visits her in September, and once in February, they pruned and mulched the roses together. Each time he leaves he is usually carrying a few things of his father's. He had a briefcase and a raincoat this last time. He was beaming and he came over to the fence to show me and to thank me for helping "my mom." That's what he calls his stepmother. I think to myself this is decent, kind of him, really, to refer to her as his mom, since she has told me he is the closest to a son she will probably ever have. I tell him it's no trouble. I just do her lawn when I do my own.

But mowing my neighbor's lawn has gotten to be something I actually look forward to, I admit. I like to make a swirling green current the way I cut the grass, so the lawn has a river, an invisible river of pattern with ridges of energy cut right where I've moved my body along behind the mower. I can work up a good rhythm. There's a kind of hum running inside me so pleasurably I forget what time it is, or if the darkness is falling, as it often does. I'm moving with the current under the boughs of the cedar trees. When I'm finished and have shut off the mower, my neighbor comes out of the house to stand next to me.

I've never told her about the dream I have repeatedly, in which she crosses to me on the freshly cut lawn and holds out one of Mr. Woodriff's already-tied neckties, loosened to slip over my head. I bend my head down, but even so, she still has to reach up. It's like I'm receiving a medal after performing in some amazing exhibition of human will and daring, only I can't think what I've done to deserve this tie coming over my head. I feel ordinary and humbled as the tie slips down to my shoulders, but my neighbor seems so sure about what she's doing that I just give over. I go ahead and cinch the necktie, sliding the knot under my Adam's apple. It's then I feel an unexpected moment of satisfaction. Like the already-tied necktie, this peacefulness also seems somehow to have been ready for me.

In the dream I have the sense that Mr. Woodriff is advising me, telling me it's okay to leave some things to others, the way he managed his closetful of neckties. I wake up feeling greatly calmed and included, remembering how he let me help him that day. Then I realize this is the same feeling I have after I've cut my neighbor's lawn. We admire the lawn together awhile, taking silent note of its rushing, a low murmur in the leaves of the big maple near the garage. After a minute or two she thanks me, but neither of us goes anywhere. We survey the sweep and eddies of the lawn together, and for a moment a stupendous calm falls over that small corner of the world. It's then I take leave of her and go back to my own house to fix the evening meal. The same way she must be doing over there.

The legendary Calamity Jane is almost entirely the creation of the romanticists in need of a tragic Western heroine. These writers paid little attention to the known facts, but in this they had the full-hearted encouragement of Calamity Jane herself.

Rain

Flooding

Your

Campfire

Mr. G.'s story, the patched-up version I'm about to set straight, starts with a blind man arriving at my house. But the real story begins with my working ten-hour days with Norman Roth, a blind man who hired me because he liked my voice.

My job included typing, running errands, filing, and accompanying the blind man to court. But most of the time was spent reading out loud to him from police reports. We were working Research and Development for the Seattle Police Department.

Those days, before qualified people like Norman got real consideration, a blind man working for the police was definitely rare, not to say bizarre. But they left us alone, those other researchers and developers. They gave us a cubicle with no windows and shut the door. That was okay by Norman. He liked it fine and I guess I did too. It was my job, after all.

Norman was a chain-smoker. He had a little chain he pulled from his vest pocket and rattled the first time he broke the news. Then he laughed and lit up. Sometimes I could barely make out the silo on the State Fair calendar behind him. But we did okay. We listened to each other's stories, tried to make work interesting, even brought treats to share. Frequent breaks made sense, once we realized nobody was keeping tabs on us. What I'm saying is, we edged into friendship during those ten-hour days.

After our work at the SPD wrapped up in the early seventies, Norman and I corresponded by tape, and once in a blue moon we'd telephone. A while later he got married and passed through a series of low-grade jobs for the Feds. Then, with the help of his wife, Caroline, who was sighted, he quit the government and started his own business.

I'd made a few wild swerves and ended up moving back East, working at a gas company and living with Ernest, who, for the most part, understood a woman's life hadn't started the minute he walked through the door. He knew about my ten-year friendship with the blind man I'd known in Seattle. So, when Norman came out East and called from New York City to arrange a visit, Ernest didn't make a big deal. He griped a little, sure. But that's in the nature of things. It probably made things easier that Norman was in mourning after his wife's death, and that his visit to me was part of his journey to see her relatives. Ernest could hardly object under these circumstances.

Norman and I had a saying in our Seattle days when things bummed us out. "Rain flooding your campfire," we'd say to each other, and whatever it was didn't seem so bad. But there was no one to say that to after I read Mr. G.'s version of Norman's visit. All I could think of was the tender, painful things about my friend Mr. G. hadn't known to tell.

Gallivan is Mr. G.'s real name. He and I work grave-yard at the gas company. I have a repertoire of sixties songs I hum, two of which will send him flaming from the room—"Maggie May" and "It's All Over Now." I'm also an intermittent whistler. If Mr. G. were doing the work he's paid to, my habits wouldn't be a problem. But most of the time he's hammering at his novels and stories on the secretary's old Selectric. Nothing he writes gets published. Does that stop him? He claims he needs a breakthrough with the editors. My opinion is, he'll type till kingdom come, inflicting this stuff endlessly on his unfortunate fellow workers.

If Mr. G. were an out-and-out liar I would have more respect for his storytelling. As it is, he can't imagine anything unless he gouges himself with the truth, and that makes it hard for those who know what really happened. The result is the "marble-cake" effect. Aside from this, he's not an altogether bad guy. He did, by default, invite Norman to dinner when he appeared a day earlier than expected.

Ernest and I were just locking the front door, heading to Mr. G.'s, when the phone rang. It was Norman. He was at the train station, wondering where I was.

"I'm here in my house," I said.

"Oh dear," he said. I could picture him touching his watch with the days of the week nubbed into it—a watch he no longer owned, as it turned out.

"It's Friday," I said. "You're a day ahead of me, Norman. No problem," I lied. "I'll be right down to get you."

I managed to sound cheerful, practically eager. I phoned Mr. G., who said it would be fine to bring Norman to dinner. Ernest had beefed up a drink, switched on the TV, and stretched out on the couch, so I decided to drive to the station alone.

"Ernest," I said. "Please clear those keepsakes and stack the throw rugs on the porch." I was still worrying about electric cords and faulty railing as I pulled out of the drive.

When Norman married, I'd been grateful for his having Caroline, but I also liked her on her own ground, not just because she was devoted to my friend. I'd been sorry, for both their sakes, that I was so far away when she fell ill. Norman told me in one of his calls before her death more than I could absorb about the cancerous brain tumor that was taking her from him. There'd been months of deterioration. Near the end, we'd recalled better times, one early in their courtship when I'd taken them camping at Mount Angeles. Before she lost her voice, his wife had been looking at the pictures with him, describing them to Norman. The photos of that long-ago trip gave them solace, he said. He used that word, "solace."

"Strange, her losing her voice like that," Norman told me. "Oh, she knew everything. Just couldn't make a peep." He said she would give him little pressure signals on his hand—yeses and noes to questions he formulated. "I had to talk for both of us. 'Want to try some physical therapy?' I'd ask. 'Okay, sure,' I'd say. 'Need that pillow under your shoulders? All right. The window up? Some fresh air?' "

When I arrived at the station, Norman was standing next to a small black valise.

"Norman!" I said, locating myself in front of him. We

embraced, then he stepped back, leaned forward and fumbled for my face.

"I'm so humiliated," he said, then planted a kiss hard on my jaw. "A day early! I could evaporate!"

"Now, now," I said. I took his arm and he picked up the valise. "You're here. That's what matters. I just wish I'd had the whole day to look forward to you."

We made our way as far as the taxi stand when he stopped, let go of my arm, set the valise down and took an object the size of a deck of cards from his shirt pocket. "Look at this. My new computerized watch. I guess it was misprogrammed on the day." He pushed a switch activating a voice: "Sat-ur-day: Fi-ive for-ty-ni-en and fif-ty seconds." A melodious bell tone sounded.

"That's something," I said. He returned the voice-clock to his pocket, took up his bag and we made our way to the car. I situated him, stowed the valise, then got behind the wheel. "Good to see you, Norm!" I said, and patted him on the arm.

I genuinely liked this man and was very moved by the fact he'd taken the trouble to visit me at this difficult time in his life. "Don't you worry about a thing," I assured him. "Mr. Gallivan says you're welcome to join us for dinner. He's a writer," I told Norman. "He's written six novels and three books of nonfiction. Right now he's suffering writer's block, so he's taking up slack by entertaining people from work."

Norman was fresh from having visited his dead wife's relatives in Vermont. (Mr. G. places them in Connecticut.) Visiting me was his last stop before returning to Seattle. He confessed he didn't miss Caroline as much now as he'd thought he would. "It's a terrible thing," he said. "But true." He was fingering my dashboard, trying to tell the make.

"This isn't the same car you had," he said.

"That one bit the dust long ago," I said. "This is a 1973 Beetle."

MR. G.'S STORY begins as we get out of the car at my house and I help Norman up the steps. The narrator sees his wife (that's me!) gripping the arm of the blind man, guiding him toward the house. Here he is, catching a view of the wife in a moment of intimacy with a blind man.

Norman leaned on my arm as we took the steps. "That one nearly got me," he said. On the porch I held back the screen and asked Norman to step inside.

Ernest wasn't around. I set the valise at the end of the couch, moved some newspapers, and Norman sat down. In no time I'd stepped into the kitchen and mixed a couple of Bloody Marys.

Soon we began to reminisce. We sipped our drinks and called up names at the Police Department—Barbara Dukes, a woman officer we'd liked—still and forever, we imagined, in Juvenile. Then I mentioned Sergeant Smiley, in the Bad Checks Department.

"Oh, you mean *Chuckles*," Norman said, arching his chest and leaning back to laugh. "Gee, it's so dark in here I can't *feel* where I'm going," Norman used to say, then purposely bang into a file cabinet. He used to do that a lot, change things from sighted terms to hearing, smelling, or touching. Then he'd laugh his big, booming laugh.

Norman was trying to locate an ashtray on my coffee table. I placed one under his hand. I'd nearly forgotten Ernest when he came down the stairs. Before he could sit down, I motioned him toward us.

"Norman," I said to my friend, "this is Ernest, the man

I live with. Ernest, Norman Roth." Norman got to his feet. His hand came up like a pistol, thumb cocked. Ernest looked at the hand, then took it. He was not thrilled to have a blind man in his house. (Mr. G. at least has that much right.)

"Pleased to meet you," Norman said brightly, furrowing his brow as if straining to see. He pumped Ernest's hand like the Tin Man in *The Wizard of Oz*, then reached to relocate his place on the couch before stiffly sitting down again.

"Heard a lot about you," Ernest said.

"Nothing too bad, I hope," Norman said. "I wonder, could I get a light off you, Ernest, if you're still up?"

Ernest fished for his lighter and handed it to me. I flicked it, then touched the flame to the cigarette Norman held between his lips. He inhaled deeply. Smoke issued from his mouth and nose. Once he was satisfied he couldn't be seen, Ernest took a chair near the couch.

"How was the train ride?" he asked. He lifted his bourbon and took a swig.

"Swell, just swell," Norman said. "After I got the porter trained to bring me drinks, it was very pleasant." He put a hand awkwardly inside his jacket lapel and kept it there. He smiled, nodded silently. Suddenly he remembered his cigarette ash. He withdrew the hand and started pinching the air above the coffee table. When he'd located the rim of the ashtray, he knocked his ash expertly and smiled toward the unknown room, obviously enjoying the fact he was on top of things. He lifted his drink and took a long draw.

I should say he's not blond, as Mr. G. describes him. He's bald, except for close-shaven sideburns and a band of hair at the back of his neck. Because his eyes are clouded he's always seemed balder to me than he is. From the start I felt invisible when Norman looked at me. A person could stare back as long as they wanted and not meet the smallest glimmer in those eyes.

"Ever see one of these?" Norman said, offering his voice-watch in Ernest's direction. "Little bugger got me here a day early."

Ernest reached across the coffee table. "Six-twen-ty-four and ni-en sec-onds," the watch said, then the cherubic bell sounded.

"Great little gadget," Ernest said. "How much did it set you back?"

"Got a deal from the Bureau for the Handicapped," Norman said. He waited for the watch to touch his hand, then slipped it into his pocket.

"Good to see the taxpayers' dollars helping a few needful sorts," Ernest said. I shot him a shut-up-or-I'll-kill-you look, but he just grinned.

"We'd better head to Gallivan's," I announced. Anything to get Ernest's mouth full of food before he started wishing out loud a little federal aid would come his way. We hadn't finished our drinks, so Ernest dropped our glasses into the slots of a carry-out and headed for the car while I helped Norman.

Mr. G. lives in a brick duplex. Shrubs crowd the walkway, but Mr. G. has clipped a little passageway to his door. The whole neighborhood's a mess—cans, bottles, old newspapers, yards knee-high in grass. Naturally Mr. G. does not mention this in his account.

When Mr. G. opens the door he has on what I call his uniform—a yellow shirt, green tie, khaki trousers. He's worn these at the gasworks the three years I've known him. He probably likes not having to interrupt his thoughts with decisions while he dresses every morning.

"Welcome," Mr. G. says to Norman. "Nice you could

join us." I stepped to the side so Norman could give Mr. G. one of his pile-driver handshakes.

Ernest squeezed Mr. G.'s arm conspiratorially as he walked past into the living room. Mr. G. positioned my two fellow workers in front of Norman. They each met his grip and stepped back: Sal Fischer—the soft-spoken foreman on swing shift, there with his old Lab, Ripper, and Margaret, a secretary who was dating Sal, pretty in a blue cotton print dress with red tulips along the hem. Ripper nosed Norman's crotch, then grudgingly allowed himself to be petted.

"Smell that food, Norm?" Gallivan said. "We're in the homestretch."

Norman rolled his head toward the kitchen. "I'd know pork roast at fifty paces." He fixed a grin on his face like someone waiting for his picture to be snapped.

"Amazing," Mr. G. said. "You're close. It's back ribs, made with my special Texas barbecue sauce."

I situated Norman on a sturdy chair and went into the kitchen. I knew the dinner had been on hold until we got there, so it was decent of Mr. G. to smooth that over. I could hear Norman's voice above the others. Mr. G. had begun to question him about the free availability of "talking records" for lazy but sighted readers.

"My father *can* read," Mr. G. was saying, "but he doesn't. He might listen, though. If he could just plug in a novel while he shaves or tidies up."

Norman was acting very deaf.

"Ernest," I called into the living room. When he came into the kitchen, drink in hand, I gave him the platter of ribs.

"What're you doing?" he asked. "This isn't your kitchen." His eyes had that glassy look of someone warmed up for a party long before it had started.

"I know," I said. "I'm taking charge." I dished up coleslaw and beans. I filled the water pitcher, then went into the living room to announce we were ready. By the time the others wandered into the dining room, Ernest was seated.

"Here, Norman," Mr. G. offered. "Sit next to me. I want to hear about your Independent Management Enterprises."

"Oh, that's finished," Norman said. "Now that my wife's gone, I don't have the heart for it."

"I'm sorry, I didn't catch that," Mr. G. said and cocked his head. "Gone?" He held his eyes on Norman a moment, then unbuttoned his cuffs, rolled up his sleeves, and forked a side of ribs onto his plate. He raked another portion onto Norman's, then reached across him to serve Margaret, who kept trying to catch my attention, as though I should signal her what to do.

Norman lifted a row of ribs from his plate and began to chew vigorously. He leaned over the table so as not to drop anything onto his lap or the floor. We got into some serious eating. Bones clacked onto our plates. I imagined Norman heard that sound. I'd been enjoying how, without the slightest concession to the sighted world of manners, he licked barbecue sauce from his fingers, when suddenly he pushed his chair back and stood up uncertainly.

"Where's the loo, if you'd be so kind?" The British accent he put on made his question sound refined, almost invisible. He asked it roughly in the direction of the light fixture, then took a jerky step into the table, like one of those TV monsters who can see to kill, but that's about it. Margaret looked alarmed, as if he might stoop and carry her off. I got to my feet and led Norman down a hallway.

"The facility's to your right," I said. "I'll wait for you, Norm." I switched on the light for him, realized what I'd done, then flicked it off.

I heard Norman's watch go off, then the water running. It ran a long time. When he didn't come out, I listened harder. I could hear sobbing. I stood there thinking what to do, then knocked softly and the sobbing stopped. I thought he might really break up if I took his arm when he came out, so I went back to the table and asked Ernest to go get him.

"What'd he do, fall in?" Ernest said. He moved the bones on his plate to one side and helped himself to more ribs. Then he looked wearily at me, pushed his chair back and got up.

In a little while I could hear Ernest and Norman bumping along the hallway. It was then that Ripper broke from under the table. He scrabbled across the hardwood floor and began to tear at Norman's trouser leg. Norman would have been hearing a lot of growling and slavering at his ankles. Sal cursed, rose from his chair, and caught Ripper's collar. He pulled so hard he collided with the table edge. For Norman it was a yowl, then a series of thuds spiced with cursing. He looked strangely disheveled with his trouser cuffs askew.

When things had settled down, I mentioned a TV special I didn't want to miss, thinking to head us home. "It's on the continuing threat of nuclear war," I said. Mr. G. threw down his napkin and said, "I'd love to see that. My TV's on the fritz. We need to face up to the horror of what *could* happen, even if we can't do anything." Mr. G. deftly turned the cleanup over to Margaret and Sal, and followed us through the undergrowth to the car.

"I want to hear about your dreams," Gallivan said to

Norman as he slid into the back seat beside him. "Is it true that if someone were throwing, say, a lemon meringue pie at you in a dream—you'd experience the taste of 'lemon pie'; then you'd feel sticky meringue all over your face?"

Norman rocked back and forth against the seat. "That's about it, kiddo."

None of the dinner scene just described or the lemon-pie remark makes it into Mr. G.'s story. He also removes himself entirely from a scene in which, purportedly, a blind man, plus a husband and wife, watch a TV program and the wife falls asleep. One thing is true: I did fall asleep. But not before I'd taken Norman and his bag upstairs to the spare room. I plumped his pillows and helped him locate an ashtray and towels I'd placed on a nightstand. Then he sat on the bedside, tipped his head back and his blind eyes ranged off toward a Mexican vaquero, a velvet wall hanging my brother had bought me in Juárez.

"Caroline's mother," he said. "I think I could have gotten through it okay except for her."

"We'll have a good talk tomorrow, like old times," I said. The vaquero in his spangled sombrero, poised to give a bull the slip, begged me to mention him, but I didn't. Norman could get along without him.

"I just want to tell you this one part," Norman said. He let his head roll back, righted himself and leaned forward. "After the biofeedback petered out, Caroline's mother'd do things like have her refuse drugs for the pain. 'She says she doesn't want those pills,' her mother would say. 'She says she can handle it. Can't you, honey?' I mean, imagine me watching someone *else* put words into Caroline's mouth."

I thought about the word "watching," how some of my friends would have tittered at this. But I knew Norman *had* "watched." He gave keen attention to details. I remembered the last time I'd heard him say the word "watched." "I love to *watch* the flames"—he'd said. Our campfire was blazing on that long-ago mountainside and the heat of the flames danced against our faces. We watched.

I stood up and eased my hand under Norman's elbow. I wanted to hear him out, but knew it wasn't the time.

"We'll sit a little, then say good night," I said, as we entered the living room. I coached Norman past my big paradise palm toward the couch. Mr. G. was fine-tuning the set. Ernest had his shoes up on the coffee table. I seated Norman, then told him I was going upstairs to get ready for bed. I glanced at Ernest, who jiggled his eyebrows when he heard me say "bed."

After I'd changed I came downstairs and took a place on the couch near Norman. He'd begun to nod, but I couldn't tell if he was napping or just agreeing to something he was thinking. Mr. G. was banging ice cubes in the kitchen. Ernest lifted his glass in my direction and gave me the old glitter-eye, so I flipped my robe, hoping it would accelerate getting upstairs. But the TV was on and Norman suddenly asked a question.

"What's he mean, 'limited nuclear war'? How limited is it if they obliterate Europe?"

"Next war you're fried, eyeballs and all," Ernest said.

"Or gassed or shot," Norman said. "For once I'm glad I'm not able-bodied."

Mr. G. returned, a drink in each hand. He'd loosened his tie and I could tell he was on the scent of "material." An aircraft carrier as big as three hotels moved heavily across the screen. My eyes were shutting down and I'd be asleep sitting up in no time, but I couldn't seem to move. Ice cubes were clinking in glasses. *Norman hears those ice cubes,* I thought hazily, and felt close to him in the old ways, those times I'd had to think what he needed for an entire day. I also recalled helping him across a log over a river as we'd headed up Mount Angeles, how scared Caroline had been. But Norman had trusted me on the unsteady log, the river rushing and deep ten feet below us. That trust still held a place with me, that's why Norman is here, I thought.

The word "capability" occurred repeatedly in the voice from the TV. Then I heard Norman ask Ernest to find a piece of paper and some scissors. I must have dozed because when I woke up, my robe had fallen open. Ernest, Mr. G., and Norman were bent over the coffee table. Mr. G. had Norman by the hand and was moving his fingers over a piece of paper. "That's the nose right there," Mr. G. was saying. "Feel that?"

"What are you doing?" I asked.

"Helping him *see* a missile," Ernest said. "We cut one out of paper."

"Flash," Norman said. "That means a sudden burst of light."

Ernest laughed. He shook Mr. G.'s arm. "Hey, try cutting out a flash."

"But the word 'light.' What does that really mean to you?" Mr. G. asked Norman. "I mean, I could say 'a sudden flash of sagebrush' and it would be all the same, wouldn't it?"

"A nuclear flash would be blinding," Norman said. "In some things, I'm ahead of you."

As Mr. G. tells it, the program was on cancer hot spots in the body, so they weren't examining the cutout of a missile at all, but a drawing of the stomach. Mr. G. ties this in nicely with the death of Norman's wife. The narrator in Mr. G.'s story, an inarticulate sort, experiences blindness through his blind visitor. Mr. G. says he's considering a twist in his rewrite, maybe bringing in Norman's intrusive mother-in-law.

What really happened was that I cinched my robe shut, got up and switched off the TV. "Enough's enough," I said. "Good-bye, world."

I left the three of them sitting there and went upstairs. It was a hot, muggy night. I took off my robe, then my nightgown, and got into bed. I could hear Ernest on the stairs, but he didn't come into the bedroom. Then I heard voices outside on the lawn. It was summer and the screens were on, so whole good-night love scenes from the neighborhood teenagers, or even lovemaking noises from the nearby houses, would drift through the windows.

"Where have you been?" I asked when Ernest finally came into the bedroom.

"Having a cigarette," he said.

"Where's Norman?"

"Nobody ever told your blind man the constellations, so Gallivan's doing it. Out there telling him the stars." He undressed, put on his pajamas, and got into bed. Soon he reached over and began patting my hair the way he does when he wants to get something started. Then he discovered I was naked and his motions took on another eagerness.

"How's Gallivan getting home?" I asked, paying him no mind.

"It's a great night for walking," Ernest said.

I threw back the covers, got up and went over to the open window, raised the shade and looked down. There was Mr. G. holding Norman's arm over his head as if he'd won a prize fight. They were illuminated from above by the street lamp.

"This here, see? That's the Big Dipper." Mr. G. moved Norman's arm in an arc. "The Dipper's handle is along there."

I couldn't see the stars. Nobody could, because the sky was overcast. I'd looked at stars since childhood, but never learned much about constellations. Oh, I knew some bore the names of animals, and Greek gods, and I might have found Orion if my life depended on it, but so far it hadn't.

"What stars?" I asked. "Ernest, take a look at this."

Ernest got out of bed. He stood behind me and leaned over my shoulder. Two men stood in our front yard with their arms raised. Mr. G. was calling out the stars like a stationmaster.

Ernest cupped his hands around my breasts and rested his chin behind my ear. We saw Mr. G. lead Norman into the middle of the street. Then a siren went off somewhere. I began to think how strange it is that stars are silent. What if each star made the smallest noise—say the insistent tone of Norman's watch—what an enormous din would pour down on us!

Mr. G. had turned Norman in another direction entirely. Headlights of a car rose like a strange bloated moon over the hill, beamed on them a moment, then swept precariously down another street. Ernest and I got back into bed, but we could still hear them. It would be just like Gallivan, in some jaunty hail-fellow-well-met good-bye, to forget totally Norman was blind, and simply strike out for home. Which is exactly what he did.

I had wanted to stay awake until Norman was safely inside and in his room—but Ernest's hands began to move over me until my shape seemed to rise and drift from the room. I don't even remember when I closed my eyes.

Somewhere in my uneasy sleep, I saw Norman standing in the front yard. His face was turned skyward and he was holding on to a tree as if he were afraid some force might pull him from the earth. The sky inside his mind must have seemed hugely populated after all the instruction he'd taken.

About then I jerked awake. It was so warm in the house I didn't bother to put on my robe, just made my way downstairs in the dark. My dream had uncannily intersected the real—Norman was there under the trees. I unlatched the screen and went down the porch steps toward him. I didn't speak, but I had a feeling he knew I was there. The houses were dark now and the maples, in a light breeze, made a soft rushing above us which could just as well have belonged to the stars, visible now and blinking calmly down.

I should have been cold outside in the night air, but I wasn't. I heard myself say something consoling as I stood beside Norman. I felt completely unconcerned that I was naked, as if I were somehow still dreaming and protected by the blindness of the world to dreams. It was one of those crossover moments where life overflows, yet somehow keeps its shape. Norman let go of the tree and said, "That you?" "Yes," I said. Then I slipped my hand under his elbow and, as if the entire world were watching and not watching, I guided our beautiful dark heads through a maze of stars, into my sleeping house.

In captivity, hummingbirds seem to enjoy engaging in combat with other hummingbirds during the day, only to set their grievances aside at night, when they sleep close to each other, often no more than an inch or so apart.

The

Mother

Thief

With the electric attentiveness of a deer in headlights, Jeanette fixed on the contents of the six-page letter. It had been composed by her cousin Felicia while she and her live-in love, Dave, had been on a camping trip in Canada. The envelope exuded the sweet smell of kerosene and, as she read, cinders from their campfire sifted from the pages. It was the first letter written by lantern light Jeanette had ever received. She assumed that the primitive lighting and general surround of darkness, inhabited by wildlife, had contributed to the toothy nature of the letter's contents.

"Dave is not a drug addict," Felicia insisted in a script which flickered at an uphill slant. "This untruth, spread so thoughtlessly to the family," Felicia believed, "must have started with you." Furthermore, Felicia maintained that any damage to a borrowed chain saw had been purely accidental, and if Jeanette had not been prepared for damage, she shouldn't have lent it.

"Dave," Felicia continued, "takes nothing stronger than aspirin or Tylenol. An occasional Advil." There was a coda about the nature of unconditional love, which Jeanette guessed had been meant to reassure her, but which tasted strangely, given the rest. Finally, Felicia cautioned her once again about "thoughtless and gossipy remarks to others."

Still and all, gossip had become the family's order of the day—ever since Felicia had been contacted by her birth mother. The family had been moving vicariously toward the reunion of birth mother and daughter, as if it were happening to each of them. Jeanette, however, felt the whole affair had thrown the family out of alignment. Prior to this, Felicia, because she was adopted, had belonged to them all, but now she seemed to be moving beyond them. Jeanette's participation in this new dimension of Felicia's life had been complicated by their falling-out over the borrowed chain saw.

Jeanette hadn't minded lending the saw. It had belonged to her father and had been given to her after her father's death. But when it came back with the chain broken, it unexpectedly acquired fresh stature in relation to the loss of her father. Jeanette made the mistake of mentioning the incident to one of her mother's three sisters, who then mentioned it to Felicia's adoptive mother, Ricky, who took the matter straight to Felicia. By this time, whatever Jeanette had said was significantly embellished by the family penchant for drama and chaos.

Jeanette had been stung to the core by Felicia's punitive campfire letter. When she told her mother about it, she was shocked to learn her mother had received a copy of the letter. Felicia had also mailed a copy to Aunt Hallie, the cousins' mutually favorite aunt—the person Jeanette believed most likely to have speculated about Dave's post-Vietnam drug habits. Aunt Hallie's own son had been sent for drug rehabilitation and it had been such a blow to her that she now saw drugs everywhere. When she visited someone's house she would disappear into the bathroom. The muted snapping of plastic containers, as they spilled from medicine cabinet to sink, would signal her inventory. Aunt Hallie could tell you what everyone in the family was "on."

Jeanette felt betrayed and isolated by the circulation of what she would have considered personal correspondence. Had Felicia really imagined she could turn Jeanette's own mother against her? *And* Aunt Hallie? She smiled to realize her mother must be taking pleasure watching her daughter and adopted niece try to outdo each other in their ministrations toward her. Ultimately Jeanette arrived at the conclusion that Felicia was a woman starved for mothers. Ever since Aunt Ricky and Uncle Jack, Felicia's adoptive parents, had retired to a small town in Oregon near their natural daughter Phyllis, Felicia had been quietly bereft. Now it seemed her cousin had converted her grief into action and was aggressively shoring up her familial bulwark by attempting to appropriate Jeanette's mother, both in sympathy and fact.

However hurt she'd been by Felicia's recent actions, Jeanette still regarded her as the sister she'd never had. Their misunderstanding had unexpectedly forced Jeanette to experience what it was to be outside the family enclosure, something her cousin might have experienced more often than she'd been aware. To set things right, she'd invited Felicia to Sunday brunch. The meeting, at one of the town's more upscale restaurants, was timed to follow Felicia's return from Miami. By then Jeanette knew her cousin would have encountered her birth mother and there would be plenty to talk about.

Jeanette and Felicia hugged each other in the entry of the restaurant, but it was a fainthearted hug that lingered awkwardly as they waited for the hostess to notice them. Not a moment too soon she maneuvered them through the busy islands of tables to an empty booth. They slid onto vinyl-cushioned seats that gave sad little puffs of air as they settled. The bustle of the restaurant quickly drew them in, enclosed and protected their meeting. They'd barely glanced at the extensive menu when Felicia's account of her birth mother began to tumble forth with the excited onrush of a waterfall. From sheer force, all else receded.

"I woke up to find this woman rubbing my feet!" Felicia said, as if a python had cinched her ankles. "Imagine! I'd just met her the night before and she takes this liberty."

Because Jeanette was particularly sensitive in her feet, she felt her toes draw inward in her white slip-ons. The pressure of Felicia's story caused the cousins to choose their breakfasts hurriedly while their waitress hovered.

"Totally weird," Felicia said, rushing on. "She asks, 'Do you mind if I give you a massage?' and I say I'm not exactly comfortable with that; no, I'm really *not*. She tells me I don't know what I need, that *she's* the mother and *she* needs to 'bond' with me. She says, 'You were just days old when I last set eyes on you.' She tells me she has to rub my fingers and toes, to get the *feel of me* back into her."

"And you let her?" Jeanette asked, reappraising her cousin. Felicia had always been so take-charge that this scene refused to include the collected person sitting across from her, who didn't break stride in her account, even as their breakfasts were placed before them.

"The woman," Felicia said, "Bernadine's her name, but now I call her 'the woman.' She says my body came out of her body and she needs to touch me *all over*. 'I want to give you an all-over body massage,' she tells me. For two years she's been reading books on birth mothers getting back with their children. But she came up with this idea herself—a full body massage."

"You let her?" Jeanette asked incredulously.

"I kept saying I wouldn't be comfortable," Felicia said, an edge to her voice. "But she'd say something else. Not persuasion, really, but like it was going to happen, no matter what I said. Then I'd say *again* I wouldn't be comfortable. Don't ask me how—before I knew what was what, she got me to take off my clothes and lie on the floor. There's a blanket under me. I'm in the buff, not a stitch over my hind end, and she's oiling me like she's basting a roast. I mean I was in the oven and cooking." Without taking her eyes from her cousin, Jeanette lifted a small pewter pitcher and absently drizzled hot syrup over her pancakes.

Later Felicia would tell Jeanette's mother, as if to shield herself in aftermath, that she'd never allowed her birth mother to so much as lay a pinky on her. The discrepancy in the stories caused Jeanette and her mother to break into an unexpected round of hilarity. It was contagious. They didn't even know exactly why they were laughing, but they laughed until tears ran down their cheeks. Jeanette thought maybe it was relief, pure and simple, that Felicia had her evasions and moments of unaccountable surrender too. Still, their sympathies remained firmly with her. They saw that whatever she told others, it was important to Felicia that her birth mother had accepted her in the moment, no matter how unsympathetically she might present the woman afterward. They also saw that the presence of the birth mother had been so powerful that she'd managed to drive Felicia into a panic of capitulation, and this reluctant giving over, as much as anything, had managed to alienate Felicia from the birth mother, at least for the time being.

"Why'd you stay at her house in the first place?" Jeanette asked her cousin.

"I didn't want to insult her before I even knew her," Felicia said. "Hospitality was the first thing she wanted to give me. I thought okay, I didn't take anything from you all these years, it's okay to accept this. Wrong," Felicia said. "Dead wrong."

"Why didn't you go to a motel when she started getting weird?" Jeanette asked, thinking what she might have done.

"The plane ticket took everything I'd saved," Felicia said, as if stating the obvious.

"You're lucky she didn't try to spoon-feed you icky yellow squash from a baby-food jar," Jeanette said.

"Pablum," Felicia said, picking up the tease. "I should have screamed for my pablum!" Now they were giggling like schoolgirls and Jeanette began vigorously to slice her pancakes into bite-sized pieces. Felicia spooned salsa over her omelette, then speckled it with Tabasco for good measure.

"What's scary is how reasonable she sounded. She told me my father was Colombian. (Don't tell Aunt Hallie!) He came to the States to train for his family's hotel business back in Cartagena. He'd wanted to adopt me on his own, take me back to Colombia, but the woman, Bernadine, was too furious. My birth mother discovered he'd not only cheated on his Colombian wife, but on her, too. She told me his having a wife was one thing, but she couldn't forgive him for making it with this 'two-bit hussy' who slung hash in the cafeteria. So the big news for me is that I got adopted out by default. Bernadine caught my birth dad at sexual Ping-Pong, then dumped him *and* me. Now when I do something nuts I have to wonder if it's the Bernadine in me," Felicia said. She tore off a hunk of bread from the sourdough loaf and glanced furtively around the restaurant at customers dressed in their Sunday best.

"Before, when I didn't know my bloodline," Felicia said, "I could just be once-in-a-while-crazy, like I'd invented it. If I blow a fuse now, it goes back in my mind to this woman. Bernadine. I have to wonder now if it's my genes. Maybe I'm stuck with it."

"You must feel lucky she gave you away to Aunt Ricky and Uncle Jack," Jeanette said quietly.

"We're talking big-time luck," Felicia said, her green eyes widening. "Luck so good not even the Irish have it. This woman is rubbing my butt crack with almond oil. Is this supposed to calm me down, or what? It's not to be believed. She says, 'If you were my son and you were a Sicilian bandit who'd been shot at my feet, I'd love you so much I'd lick your blood out of the dirt.' I mean, we're talking *behavior* here."

Jeanette felt more and more refreshed by the chaotic vibrancy of her cousin's ordeal, but she also began to marvel quietly at the simplicity of her own mother and father's coupling, their steady bearing and raising of her.

"After me, she'd had two more girls by her next man," Felicia said. "She never got a son. Maybe she was imagining I was her son. Who knows how a Sicilian bandit got into it! Remember, I don't know this woman."

They seemed to have drifted far downstream from the petty disagreement over the chain saw and Felicia's accusatory letter. Maybe when Felicia had penned the campfire letter, her "Bernadine side" *had* taken over. Strange, Jeanette thought, how one trouble could console and absolve another. Her mother would, of course, want to hear all the details. She was already thinking how to elude her probings when Felicia launched into the final episode.

"We fought like piranha, all teeth and gullet. God knows how I made it home without smacking her one. 'You can't win,' she kept telling me, 'I've been at this too long.' And she was right. She carried me into meanness farther than I've been or ever want to go again. She's obviously tanked her way through life and never taken a direct hit. I wimped home on the plane next day."

"What did Dave think about it?" Jeanette asked. She didn't know why she'd brought up Dave, except for commentary she was sure Dave would have freely volunteered, but which she couldn't chance making herself.

"He's such a sweetie. He felt sorry for Bernadine when she first located me. Even went to a lot of trouble helping me imagine her pain and guilt. But he's done a one-eighty. She really stripped Dave's gears."

Jeanette hadn't realized Dave had gears. As she washed down the last of her pancake with coffee, she noticed an infidel crowd had gradually taken the tables near them, people who, rather than go to church, had obviously come straight from gardening or other less easily redeemable pursuits.

"The woman phoned after I got home and said I'd treated her *just like a man*. 'A man,' she says, 'draws you up close, then pushes you away. You have to plead and beg and worm your way back. I'm your mother and you're treating me just like a man would, making me crawl and grovel, like I don't deserve anything from you.' You could wonder what kind of men she's had, right? Then she tore out all the stops. She said, 'I pity your adopted mother.' " Felicia's eyes snapped with righteous anger. She drew herself up against the back of the booth. Jeanette located her napkin and held to it in the close quarters.

"I went totally ballistic," Felicia said with obvious pleasure. "I borrowed a page from Dave. I said, 'You fucking bitch, motherfucker, don't you *ever* call this house again. Don't you assume you know *anything* about the people who loved and raised me while you were so busy nursing your ego.'" Jeanette felt singed. She took a sip from her water glass.

"Then I got off the phone and just cried and cried, until my sides ached," Felicia said. "Dave said, 'Don't waste tears.' But I said tears are never wasted. If they don't fall, what's going to soften up the hateful meanness in this world? 'Hush up,' he told me. 'If she were here she'd probably lick those salty tears right off your cheek.' It was such a dumb remark, I started to laugh. Then he called me his little Sicilian bandit and said if it would make me feel better he'd get a job working construction and hook up with the local Mafia. After that, the whole thing seemed like the worst soap opera. But you know," Felicia said, "I hadn't fazed that woman. In ten minutes she phoned me right back, and you know what? I listened. I just shut my mouth and I heard this woman talking, calm and sweet, into my ear like there was nothing I could say to make her hate me or change her mind. What could a person do? She'd decided what she needed, and she was going to have it, come hell or high water. In a certain way she still didn't need me."

Felicia seemed to have voiced the whole of it in this last remark. She'd grown calm and now appeared more fully aware of Jeanette. "I don't do everything perfect," Felicia admitted and looked down at her hands folded on the table.

It seemed for the first time during the meal that they were speaking about their misunderstanding. Jeanette marveled at how much sympathy and genuine feeling for her cousin had replaced the sense of betrayal she'd held earlier. She even felt better about sharing her mother with Felicia. She saw that her cousin might be a long while allowing herself, even in her imagination, to accept her birth mother—if she ever did—that everything was strange and askew, not what she'd hoped for or expected. Until now, Jeanette had taken her own birth circumstances for granted. But she saw that to be born out of the body of a mother who'd loved and protected her and stayed beside her from the beginning was pure accident and more than that—a gift for which there was no deserving.

Jeanette knew her cousin had shared things with her she wouldn't have, except that they'd been in this family together since childhood. They'd gone swimming in the same rivers, raced ponies at the county fair, and as teenagers played Monopoly over the telephone long into the night. They'd been through deaths in the family and illnesses, weathered the inevitable feuds of relatives. In short, they'd lived with the closeness and harm of family in ways that had allowed them to come importantly together again now.

She listened as Felicia told her, "You know what—nothing's ever going to be the way it was before her hands got all over me in Miami." She told Jeanette she felt raw, that she needed somehow to heal, to toughen and cure, to be able for the next thing to happen, whatever it might be.

Jeanette opened her purse and placed her credit card on the table next to the bill. She heard her cousin say something about the woman's last words being "You're my sorrow, all those years when I couldn't find you . . . you were my sorrow." Then Felicia said tersely, "I'm nobody's sorrow."

Jeanette didn't blame her cousin for wanting to be more than a sorrow. But she knew that when you got to the bottom of most troubles, sorrow figured into it. She herself had just passed in one side of sorrow and out the other.

The smell of freshly baked bread made her think to order a loaf for her mother. While they waited, Felicia allowed as how she expected to have to deal with Bernadine "the rest of my life."

"Surely not that long," Jeanette said. Then they were laughing, almost like old times, only different—laughter with a halo of sadness around it.

Felicia reached across the table and took the credit card from beside the check and stuffed it back into Jeanette's purse. Jeanette tried to pull the card to the surface, but the waitress suddenly stepped to the table and took the cash from Felicia.

As they left the restaurant and moved toward their cars, their arms fell naturally around each other's waists.

They were back to the comforting gestures of their girl-hoods. Still, a strangeness accompanied their closeness, as if a seemingly irresolvable pain had unexpectedly made a bridge for them to cross back toward each other.

Jeanette made a mental note to mention to her mother that Felicia had paid for lunch. That way her mother would know, without her having to say a word, that everything between them was fine.

[The saloon] decayed and vanished—or metamorphosed into another form.

It is only when Buddhas appear as ordinary beings like ourselves that their activities and blessings have meaning for us. Assuming ordinary forms means not only that they do not display all the noble major and minor marks of a Buddha, but also that they possess natural human weaknesses. Assuming such forms is a great kindness and consideration, because it is only in that way that they become visible and accessible to us.

A
Glimpse
of
the
Buddha

She was lost in the habitual unspiraling of her own signature when the cool, commanding voice broke through.

"You're in my place," the voice asserted with the authority of the Queen of Hearts. Ruby, who delighted in the Queen when she read to her granddaughter, considered it unlikely that the voice was addressing her.

"I haven't concluded my transaction," the blond woman behind the voice said. Ruby continued to date her check, the effort punctuated by jerks from the tethered supermarket ballpoint. When she'd taken up the pen she'd noticed a faded blonde putting items into double plastic bags where the grocery help usually stood, but she'd paid no heed. She'd assumed the woman was either a customer helping the beleaguered checker or a bona-fide employee.

"You're supposed to be back there with your basket," observed the woman. A scrawny arm pointed toward Ruby's shopping cart, behind which several shoppers had lined up with their groceries. Ruby's cart contained a few breakfast items and sandwich makings for her husband's lunch. He'd gone to buy lotto tickets at a machine and was nowhere in sight. The cart seemed strangely far away, waiting to be unloaded by the checker, who stood like a bespectacled white rabbit with her forepaws caught midair between her two customers.

Ruby turned back to the blonde, attempting to fathom what play of events had brought the woman's challenge. Perhaps if she explained . . .

"I needed to use this pen," Ruby said, displaying the white ballpoint. "I was getting my check ready, trying not to hold people up." No good. She could see the woman had taken further umbrage.

"You think you can just stand there and tap your foot in *my* place," the woman said, slipping yet another food item into a frosted bag, as if she feared contamination. "I'm not obliged to hurry just because you tap your foot."

Ruby looked at her feet, nestled in fresh cotton anklets and loafers, the sudden enemies she nonetheless depended upon. Neither had been tapping. They were both quietly supporting her in their usual let's-do-it fashion. Still, like her shopping cart, they seemed oddly a very long way off. She gazed down the front of her black gabardine raincoat, which made a tent over the scuffed twin loafers. *The accused,* she thought, and smiled tenderly toward the feet. *The mad little tappers.* When was the last time they *had* tapped? Were they secretly spreading unseen waves of discontent?

She fumbled her mind around the strange woman's accusation, that she had shown impatience while waiting. In fact, she realized, she never waited for anyone, even when she was, indeed, waiting. She dreamed. She went blank. She fell between cracks. But she never truly waited. That is, she was normally so much in her own ruminations that she seldom took note of others. She certainly didn't want anyone to *wait* for her. She considered waiting as something done by those with abbreviated inner lives. Had the woman, without realizing it, accused her of having no inner life?

Ruby stared, still uncomprehendingly, into the woman's face. The eyes were fierce in a disconnected way, full of pulsing authority that left no room for reception. She appeared quite mad.

"You can stand there, but you don't belong there," the woman said evenly.

"Look, lady, I don't know what happened to you before you got here," Ruby said, taking a grip, "but I see it upset you. I'm sorry, but I'm not your problem." She thought to rest her case, then unaccountably picked up steam. "I never saw you before this moment. I thought you worked here."

"You thought!" the woman mocked, and now it was clear she was wheeling away on some wild current that wished to lift Ruby by the roots of her hair and fling her across rooftops. Ruby could sense her own anger building in response. She tried frantically to douse it, but could only manage what she knew to be counterfeit kindness.

"You're a very disturbed person," Ruby heard herself

pronounce. "Once you get going, I can see you can't help behaving this way. I *am* sorry."

"Oh, excellent!" the woman exclaimed archly. "You don't fool me with your appalling decency. I know what you're made of. You and your *sorry!*"

Ruby looked at the checker, whose little paws extended now like an offering toward the woman to accept two twenty-dollar bills. Ruby's eyes met the checker's as she turned to the till, but she saw the bespectacled employee had no intention of interceding. She'd probably had intricate seminars, Ruby decided, which trained her simply to let customers duke it out. Any moment now she might dodge into a safety cupboard Ruby imagined to be located at knee level.

Faintly, like the strains of a solitary flute on a mountainside, she recalled her grown daughter's admonition that "each of us is in fact the Buddha," and how, if we could just realize this, "we would all treat each other with dignity." An imperious notion, Ruby had thought at the time, that each of us was an ultimate and holy being. Nonetheless, it seemed enlightened to remember that no matter how abject or infuriating another person might be, that person still represented an image torn from the greater wholeness and was, therefore, to be respected. Perhaps the blond woman represented worthiness in some yet-to-be-recognized form.

For Ruby's own purposes the biblical "Do unto others as you would have them do unto you" had seemed to cover most human relations for the past sixty years. Her daughter's Zen practice fruitfully intersected her own Christian beliefs from time to time. Still, she suspected that her daughter's "Oriental notions" sprang from a wish not to be overpowered by a certain brand of religious zealotry prominent at the moment. Ruby struggled now to put the "everyone's a Buddha" idea into practice. But something was stronger, and it took only the woman's next assertion to draw it forth.

"Arrogant and full of pride," the woman uttered, and Ruby heard a distant gavel fall as on marble. It echoed cavernously. "If you weren't so pigheaded, you'd yield." The woman's long, thin arms stretched toward the checker, who was hammering change out of tight rolls on the sharp ridge of the till. Blurting and ranting were definitely out of bounds for Ruby, but she was startled to have been pulled so far from her intended course of fair and respectful behavior. She felt suddenly and irretrievably possessed.

"So, you just want to make bad use of whoever happens to be standing next to you, do you?" Ruby found herself snapping at the supposed Buddha. "If it's anger you want, you got it. Step right up to bat." She had no idea, she realized perilously, what she might say or do next. The Buddha had her by the scruff of her neck, if her daughter's reading of things was correct. That is, when you found yourself *reactive,* her daughter believed, you might consider yourself questioned by the Buddha in some important realm. Ruby tried to calm herself. After all, if the Buddha-proposition worked both ways, she too was a Buddha. Unfortunately, she got her Zen theories completely secondhand. But wasn't it the hazard and gift of religion in general that it had operated quite well for centuries as more than a little secondhand?

"What are you going to *do* about me being in your place?" Ruby asked the blond Buddha. "You going to throw me out?" she challenged. After all, she'd never spoken to a Buddha before, especially what she now considered a *bad* Buddha. She patently didn't know how to converse with an abject ultimate. "I was going to move back to my cart earlier," Ruby lied, "but now I'm not doing anything you say." An incredible fixity and physical power rushed through her. She was as immovable and unfathomable to herself as the sphinx.

"I asked you nicely," the Buddha said, with a trace of dead conciliatory ardor which indicated it was now too late, in any case, for remedies. The Buddha's cottony hair, the color of horseradish, haloed her brilliant, inflexible blue eyes below slight fins of penciled-in eyebrows.

Ruby recalled a line of Japanese poetry her daughter was fond of quoting, especially when they had fish for Sunday dinner: "The fish, when slit open, / Reveals a Buddha it has eaten." Ruby had never investigated the fish for its Buddha on these occasions, but now she wanted to slit the woman open, right there in the supermarket, on the black runway of the checker's automated station, to see if the Buddha really *was* in there and, if so, what it had to say for itself. No more mirror-play with madwomen and shopping carts in supermarkets. She could use some visuals.

But, fish or woman or Buddha—the blonde was putting her change into her handbag and lifting her groceries.

"You're going to feel very sorry about all this when you get home," Ruby said, still thinking the answer to the woman's rude behavior, and her own unkind response, lay in some final words she might say to the Buddha inside the woman.

"No," the woman said. "No, I won't be the least bit sorry." She stepped onto the black pad that activated the automatic door and disappeared into the night.

When Ruby's husband reappeared she shouted at him and told him he was wasting his money on the lotto machine. Why had he been gone so long anyway? He'd missed everything. She'd been verbally attacked by "a crazy woman."

"I can well imagine you held your own," he said mildly as they crossed the parking lot—a remark for which she would later be obliged to punish him. He explained that he hadn't managed to get a single lotto ticket because the machine kept rejecting his money. Ruby thought of the inflexible metal tongue of the lotto machine sliding in and out with her husband's dollar bills. No Buddha. No lotto. A round of refusal and accusation.

"You're lucky that woman didn't take out a gun and shoot you," her husband said, as he settled their groceries into the trunk of the car. Ruby considered this. She'd managed to skip that usual phase of public encounters, the moment when it occurred to you that an honest dis-agreement might end with the other person pulling out a gun and blasting you out of the universe. She had been strangely fearless during the entire encounter. She and the woman had challenged each other and continued to hold their places. She'd stood up to the Buddha. If the Buddha wanted to act like an asshole, she could oblige. Still, two inflexible Buddhas—what could it mean?

When she was silent on the drive home her husband said, "You're going to be telling everybody about this for the next week."

"No, I won't," Ruby said.

"And you'll get to be right every time and she'll get to be crazy," he said, for he knew her well.

"No. I won't be right," Ruby said. There was sadness in her voice as she uttered this last. She felt, indeed, that she'd just participated in something singularly disgusting and debilitating to the entire history of human affairs, never mind the history of Buddhas. But if the woman had really been a Buddha, Ruby might at least have taken pride in feeling she'd been right not to capitulate. Perhaps a Buddha could make use of being stood up to. But a crazy woman? No, the woman would just go on being crazy, admonishing the world and the people in it to do as they were told, with little effect. Even now Ruby planned to discount the disturbing woman who was, she felt, ultimately on the order of the malfunctioning lotto machine. Nonetheless, she lay awake much of the night thinking about the woman, of what she might have said to yank her to her senses in regard to her fellow human beings.

THE NEXT day her husband went fishing for steelhead on the Elwha River with two mill-working buddies. Ruby's father had explained to her as a child that a steelhead was a fish that spent its life in salt water, but which returns to the freshwater river where it was born during the winter spawning. Then, unlike salmon, it returns to the sea. She had always admired the versatility of this fish and thought of its return to its birth-river as a kind of natural miracle.

When she heard the men arrive, Ruby came downstairs expecting to hear the usual stories of high, swift water, of bait lost to limbs or rocks, or, even worse—gill nets across the river mouth skimming their catch. Her husband had just waved good-bye to his friends and was removing his rubber waders at the door. When he saw Ruby he reached for something on the bottom step. It was wrapped in his T-shirt and he held it out to her emphatically, like something lost and retrieved.

Ruby drew back the sodden T-shirt and gazed at a beautiful silver fish. She took hold of it with a girlish squeal of delight. She was surprised her husband made no show of his own gladness at having caught it, for she knew he'd been fishing all season without so much as a bite. The returning steelhead had been flooded out at the mouth of the rain-swollen river for weeks. No one had had any luck. "Fishing's as rotten as the lotto," he'd said all season long.

She carried the light-spangled fish into the kitchen and took a curved knife from a drawer. Carefully she began to slit open the fish's belly with the blade that was sharp as a whisper. The steelhead was pale inside, pale pink, and the ribbing of white bones showed through the flesh like the hull of an empty ship. Once she'd cleaned the fish, something still remained. She spread the fleshy sides of the fish open so the light could shine in. Then her hand reached to touch a silken cache of unearthly orange eggs attached to the fish at its spine. The mass of unfertilized eggs, packed like miniature planets in their translucent sack, was slightly warm to her touch. Next she boldly examined one flat eye of the fish with a fingertip and marveled at how it withheld nothing from her. The eyes of the petulant woman at the supermarket had also held back nothing, she realized. Ruby had been unable to dismiss her. She realized she'd been on a pure and open current with the woman, no matter their failure to connect fruitfully in the immediate moment.

"There's a good high tide tomorrow," she heard her husband say. "I'm going to use those eggs to catch more fish. Don't throw them out."

"I won't," the Buddha said, and she reached her hand, speckled with silver scales, inside for the full cargo of bait.

The saloon is the dream palace of countless Walter Mittys, the fortress of Anglo machismo where masculinity extends its hide . . .

The
Poetry
Baron

He signed all mandates "The Poetry Baron." Or, if he wanted to particularly sweeten his way with Mary Beth—the department secretary since the first brick laid at the university—he would obsequiously pen, "The Little Baron" or "The Baronette."

He used a red ink pad and purchased a Chinese seal with a character on it which he later discovered meant something like "Two Dead Oars." But if anyone asked, he told them it meant "Long Life and Happiness." What was important was having a civilization behind him as old as the Chinese.

•

IN HIS poetry workshops the Baron liked to maintain the feel of a democratic organism reaching consensus, much as amoebic entities in distant committee rooms arrive at fresh terms like "the mentally challenged" or "the temporarily abled" or the "legally pernicious." The Baron often applied the latter to a new and rising class of welfare recipients who profitably aligned themselves with lawyers to form practically unbeatable teams. They had nothing to lose but time. When it came to forcing settlements out of entities as diverse as Safeway, the NRA, and Planned Parenthood, not to mention any well-heeled relatives of those on welfare, this team was wickedly effective.

He especially knew a lot about welfare mothers, since the eldest of his two daughters had been one for twenty-odd years, with the exception of a three-month hiatus when she'd opened a little hot-dog stand down at the ferry dock. All her letters began: "Dear Dad, I could sure use some money to buy . . ." And ended: "Remember, Dad, there are steps I can take if you can't find it in your heart to help me."

•

WHEN THE Baron gazed at the cherubic faces of his female students, he often thought tenderly of his daughter at eighteen, already pregnant with the child of a car thief.

One aspiring young poet, Betina Kibs, particularly appealed to him. She drew a black outline around her lips before painting them a scalding red so that the lips seemed to lift from the face and float toward him. All her poems were about getting dumped by her boyfriends, a succession of Cro-Magnons who debased and dismantled the empire of this defenseless tangle of black hair, blond lashes, golden nose rings, and chartreuse fingernails.

•

THE BARON always spoke last, after his students had sufficiently mauled the poem under discussion. Once they'd shaken out its entrails and begun to feign affection for certain turns of phrase, a "good image" or a "muscular verb action," he would frame his response with such circumspect benevolence that they were generally shamed into submission. If anyone began to jump rope with the entrails he would intercede, uttering something that was, on the surface, neutral, but which carried sufficient admonitory undertow to bring the little cretins to a standstill. Something like: "You cannot prick with straw—nor pierce with scimitar." They could mull that.

•

IN AN effort to correct what he considered an egregious and continuing neglect of female art, despite critical pretenses to the contrary, he would quote only women poets; yet anthologies which isolated the sex he scorned as "ghettoization." In order to demonstrate graphically the inequality of the canon, he commanded his students to rip from the assigned anthology all poems except those by women. The binding was so debilitated, as a result, that he passed out yarn and darning needles so the students could sew the few remaining pages together again.

Pages and pages, entire sheaves of male poetry wafted in the breeze created by their excited frenzy of tearing and yanking. Next, the Baron suggested the young poets pretend they were Russians living in the time of Anna Akhmatova under Stalin. They could turn off the heat in their student garrets, sit around in their greatcoats drinking watered-down tea and memorize the male poets they were about to discard—the easy ones, like Walt Whitman, Robinson Jeffers, or, say, Wallace Stevens's "The Idea of Order at Key West." *They,* the Baron's beloved outposts of the future, would be the repositories, the last living, breathing archives of these about-to-be-transmogrified verbal megalomaniacs.

THE STUDENTS were thrilled with the stringency of this assignment. They were all women, except for one blond chunky male student named Alfred Greenhill, who wore mulberry-colored socks and printed all his poems in block letters on cream-colored vellum paper his father supplied from England. Greenhill's father was an English novelist who went through paper the way elephants crush forests in Africa. Excesses of this sort caused strange linkages in the Baron's mind—Napoleon's memoirs scribbled onto the faces of playing cards for lack of paper on Saint Helena.

·

THE BARON'S attention focused often on Greenhill. Why was he always smiling? What drug was he taking to get that impermeable glazed-over look? The Baron felt an inexplicable strain of cruelty in his veins when he read Greenhill's poems. They reminded him of himself at that age—stinking with "mossy fronds," able oracularly to "gaze across continents," not to mention an Audenesque penchant for admonishing "the odious public." Napoleon would gladly have squandered this over-inflated Bambi with Marshal Ney's Third Corps, blasted by musket fire, cut to pieces by Russian cannonballs.

The Baron thought history, like literature, provided an integrative stimulus to daily life. Both history and literature, he believed, were capable of spontaneously regenerating the collective memory as an evolving organism. Napoleon, consequently, was never far from his thoughts.

·

THE POETRY BARON, a recovering alcoholic, drank only cranberry juice. Occasionally he energized it with a jounce of seltzer. But only occasionally. If he'd been asked how he'd managed his miraculous recovery, he would have lowered his voice to its most humble register and intoned, "Grace." But nobody asked. As a recovering drunk he was as unspectacularly sober as he'd been spectacular when to breathe was to drink.

•

Mary Beth left him a nonfat carob cupcake in his mailbox. On it, in gold, was a capital *B* with a little crown over it. She *did* understand.

•

He listened to the students recite passages by the male poets they had memorized from the disassembled anthology. After each recitation he would ask if there were lines or images that stuck in their minds. They should write those down. Then the Baron would say, "Memory *is* imagination. Simply forget all *except* those shreds and tatters. After all, that's what poetry must be—memorable. If it isn't, well then it's just a load of turkey whack."

The students stared at him in wide-eyed adulation. "The significant is always incorporated into the present. If it's important, it will reassert itself. Now, go back to your garrets and burn those torn-out pages. Make a hefty little bonfire and warm your sweet tushes over it." He was sure, he added, that something deep and enduring about the nature of art-through-time would occur to them as a result. He silently reflected on an image from an account of Napoleon, disguised as a Monsieur de Rayneval, lifting his coattails above his famous white breeches to warm his bum before a spitting greenwood fire in Warsaw.

•

Another letter had arrived from his welfare daughter, Trina. He thought it had the sweet-sour, ready-to-poison-your-picnic smell of rancid mayonnaise. Over the years she had engendered four children, each by a different man. The car thief appeared intermittently to "sponge off her," as she put it, and to baby-sit the two youngest, who were still at home but verging on becoming teenagers. The other three men came into focus from time to time.

Her "nest" would soon be empty, she wrote. She had recently conceived the idea she might adopt a Chinese baby girl, since children seemed to be her thing. Would he, her one and only, next-to-God father, consider signing papers declaring she had an inheritance coming? He might mention the bad hearts of his prematurely deceased father and grandfather. (Here the Baron paused and placed his right hand on his own chest as if to recite the Pledge of Allegiance.) Could he, in addition, verify that he intended to leave her substantial royalties to his fifteen books of poetry? (How, he wondered, should he break it to her that all but two of the books were out of print and that even these had netted a paltry eight hundred dollars?)

Her letter continued: Could he possibly have his various presses run spreadsheets of earnings for the past twenty years so future earnings could be projected? (Spreadsheets, indeed!) And, if it wouldn't be too much trouble, could she charge her round-trip plane ticket to Beijing on his credit card? The baby would, she was glad to say, travel home free. While Trina was in China ransacking orphanages for just the right baby, his ex-wife would be looking after two of Trina's "four little lambs," as his daughter persisted in referring to her collective offspring.

The Baron hated how "four" rhymed in his head with "poor." He stopped himself there.

•

BETINA KIBS was waiting outside the Baron's office when he arrived. She had baked a batch of chocolate-chip cookies and handed over a dozen, tied in her muffler. The

Baron was touched. He recalled Napoleon's Polish mistress, Marie Walewska, described as "beautiful but brainless." Betina put her to shame—was beautiful in a ruined sort of way, which was the fashion. He felt drawn to her stylistic savvy, her way of affecting an engagingly repellent veneer of a future ripe before its time.

He unlocked his office door, invited the young woman inside to a chair near his desk, and unwrapped the cookies. They were fuzzed with blue nubs of wool. He picked out one that was unaffected and began to munch. Betina suddenly started to sob uncontrollably. The Baron felt very concerned and protective, yet he knew it would be a mistake to leap up from his desk and throw his arms around her, as he had been wont to do with female students in his drunken pre-Baron days. He simply bowed his head and began to recite from Dorothy Wordsworth:

> *And when the storm comes from the North*
> *It lingers near that pastoral spot,*
> *And piping through the mossy walls*
> *It seems delighted with its lot.*

Betina appeared to take heart from the incantational rhythms of his recitation. Whatever had been oppressing her dissipated as suddenly as it had descended. The Baron ate another cookie. It was partly crumbled, as if she had carried it over a long and circuitous journey by horseback. Betina began exuberantly to recount Charlotte Brontë's portrayal of merry days at Thornfield Hall. She volunteered she'd been "devouring Brontë" for another class.

The Baron was pleased. He'd performed a kindly act. He had ratified the healing properties of literature. He had also eaten chocolate-chip cookies and managed to keep his hands to himself. After showing Ms. Kibs out, he opened his desk drawer and took a refreshing swig of cranberry juice. Ah, but where was his Caulaincourt to make him swerve off this sweet detour? Order through fluctuation, he reasoned, had carried him through many unsung campaigns. Why stop now?

•

"GREENHILL," the Baron said, jerking the despondent and melancholy souls of the entire roomful of young female poets to attention. "What's the meaning of this drivel?!"

•

THE BARON disliked committees. When he did serve, he opted for high visibility but little real responsibility and insisted on being chair. He'd recently consented to head a committee to design a memorial garden, the money to be donated by a bereft family whose son had thrown himself out a tenth-story window after being rejected by his first love.

The Baron generally fought all things nostalgic, but he conceived the idea of a modest waterfall and defended the proposal as if his Divine Majority must prevail. After their third meeting, he telephoned one recalcitrant committee member to reiterate the necessity of meditational alcoves in contemporary life. How else could the young be expected to accomplish that most important transfer of energy between the dead and the living? Between the so-called real and the possible? When his colleague disagreed with him about the waterfall, the Baron slammed the phone down on him. Anger management indeed! Blast the miserable curs with all you've got, then scrape the dead away from the gates and enter!

ONE EVENING his students could barely conceal their wry smiles as he entered the seminar room. (All his classes were held after dark since he believed poetry survived best when inferior forms of light, those lacking modulation and artifice, were at a minimum. He would have conducted class by candlelight had fire codes permitted.) The students continued to titter until he demanded to know what so amused them.

"Your mouth," Greenhill volunteered. "There's a lavender rim around your lips. Like you've been drinking wine."

The Baron raised himself slowly from his comfortable chair at the head of the long table and began to pace the room in silence, with great empire-crushing strides. Finally, when he knew their hearts in their young poet-breasts must be quaking, he stared at them as the Russian Field Marshal Kutuzov had stared down the French near the Nara River. "Cranberry juice," he said. Then strode toward the forest.

•

THE BARON read his mail. Again he had not received a Guggenheim. He dropped the puny pamphlet of winners to the floor and stomped on it. This was the fourteenth year he had applied. Perhaps his courier had been waylaid. He was certain he had enemies. He felt like the beast slouching toward coal-besmutted Glasgow when he considered the ill these traitors-against-posterity contemptuously bore him. He might have shaken them off in his usual meditational stroll at dusk along the Erie Canal, but it was mid-afternoon. He did a few vehement turns around his rose garden, trying to calm himself. He threatened inwardly to migrate to Oregon and took pleasure imagining the missives of entreaty from students and colleagues which would clog his departmental mailbox. Oregon. Hiking and blueberries. Perhaps he could set up shop adjoining a casino run by Native Americans along the Columbia. He would subsist on grants to pen a verse epic on the multi-cultural aspects of casino life.

Gradually the roses tamed his adventurous spirit with silence. He sang a few verses of an Irish air, about Napoleon trouncing the English. The refrain cheered him: *The bonny bunch of roses, oh!*

At last, benevolence was restored. He resolved to turn his resentment into nobility of spirit. He would write a pantoum using the names of all the poets who had ever won Guggenheims.

•

HE STUDIED himself in the mirror. A cranberry stain had inked itself imperfectly onto his upper lip, with a break at the apex. He thought he looked faintly Chinese, as in Charlie Chan, sans spats. He rubbed the stain with Irish Spring soap. But it would not come off. Like a workman, he now kept a thermos of cranberry juice with him at all times, even in the classroom. He learned to drink from it in such a way that a roseate circle formed around his lips.

The students had come to consider his mouth-ring an eccentricity, though some of the more devout claimed it was, like the stigmata, a sign of divine inclusion. At the end of a seminar on free verse he passed out packets of cherry Kool-Aid. "It's easy to love people for their strengths," he said. "But to love them for their weaknesses, now there rests true enlightenment. Human wisdom—*that* is the secret of poetry." A very silly look passed across Greenhill's face. No doubt he had spent the night roasting horseflesh on his saber point at some bivouac fire in the interminable falling snow. The tip of his nose was red.

TRINA HAD written to say she had the Chinese baby girl at her bosom. "Thanks, Dad, for helping me save her from that terrible rathole of an orphanage. I know she's in good health because they don't even make it to the orphanages if they're in bad health. They die, some at the hands of their own parents, and are buried in some god-forsaken unmarked place." The Baron considered Napoleon's vacant tomb on Saint Helena, shorn not only of its occupant, but of the cherished willows from which the soldiers stripped souvenir branches on the day of his burial. He felt like a stripped willow himself.

The rest of Trina's letter went on to explain that, despite his recent generosity, neither of her youngest "lambs" had winter coats, not to mention that the bristles on their toothbrushes were worn to the nubs. They were down to biscuits and porridge. Her son and daughter out on their own weren't making it either. She could use some cash. If he didn't "pony up" she would be sure to point out to her lawyer friend that it was *his* idea for her to adopt the Chinese girl, inflicting emotional guilt and further financial burdens on her. In any dispute it would be his word against hers. All his correspondence would instantly become legal documents, simply by virtue of her accusation. If he had anything he wanted to hide, well, it would just be too bad. He would be one dead poet.

The Baron refolded the letter and wrote "Ode to House Dust."

•

HE HAD begun to obsess about Betina. He thought he could smell chocolate-chip cookies everywhere. He hoped fervently to find her positioned outside his office door. Instead, the air seemed permeated by the giddy odor of horseflesh, no doubt roasted to feed the starving rabble. He stepped over bodies like cordwood, just to enter his humble retreat.

•

ONE OF the more acerbic female students reported having singed the plastic shower curtains in her apartment while burning the pages of white male poetry in her bathtub. The plastic stench had alarmed other tenants. The fire department had been called. She was about to be evicted. Did anyone need a roommate?

The Baron remarked that the price of great art was that the artist be misapprehended, publicly disparaged, and ultimately exiled. Greenhill invited the homeless student into exile with him and five male students majoring in engineering.

•

THE BARON took a long solitary walk by the Erie Canal at dusk. The pale oval face of Betina was seldom out of his mind now. His current wife simply thought his distracted air meant he was generating a new epic poem. He was. The heroine was mature and blond, to throw his wife off the scent. The outlines of limestone mountains appeared in misty passages at intervals, as on ancient Chinese scrolls. The poem would bear the enigmatic dedication "To My Beloved."

•

MARY BETH left a memo in his box. The committee for the memorial garden had been peremptorily dissolved. The parents of the dead student had withdrawn funding. The Baron mused sadly on the unrecorded demise of a waterfall. He made a note in his notebook. Later that day a snapshot of a double waterfall, labeled simply "Burney Falls," mysteriously appeared in his mailbox.

•

As IN A Chekhov story, the Baron's eyes "grew oily and rapacious" when he looked at Betina. Finally he seized a moment after class one night while escorting her to a rendezvous with yet another of her dolty boyfriends. He asked to have lunch so he could suggest strategies for getting her out of a certain rut regarding her subject matter. She accepted. The Baron went back to his office and, as if to raise a triumphal hunting horn or to sound an advance, lifted his thermos of cranberry juice to his lips.

•

"GREENHILL," the Baron roared. "You wouldn't know slant rhyme from a banana peel if you slipped on one!"

•

TRINA wrote to say her lawyer friend had informed her about something called Renewal Rights. According to Federal law, the baron's "works" written prior to 1978 belonged partly to her. It appeared, she wrote, that one-fourth, or maybe as much as one-third, of any proceeds from anthology and reprint rights, etcetera, should be coming to her. She would naturally keep this under her bonnet, since, if her younger sister were to find out, she could conceivably claim her own share. Trina wrote that his "legacy" was very important to her and to her lambs. She was glad the government was making sure she "participated" in his legacy, whether or not he intended it. This law, she pointed out, would countermand anything he might write into his will to exclude her. She was especially happy she would now benefit from his legacy, both after his death and now, while she was still young enough to enjoy spending the proceeds.

The Baron made a note to seek advice from his own lawyer friend.

•

THE POETRY BARON sent his students out over the weekend to feed the hungry at an inner-city soup kitchen. They needed to learn social responsibility. It should seep into their poems osmotically, he told them, not simply be barnacled on as an afterthought. Many of them, unlike the Chinese, had never had to share a meal dipped from the communal pot. How would they have stood up to an evening in retreat with Marshal Victor at twenty-seven below: "Frozen birds, frozen horseflesh, frozen tears."

•

HIS LAWYER friend had gone to Florida for an extended holiday. The Baron was left in the dark about Renewal Rights, although a voice on the telephone at the Writers' Defense League told him they could only apply *after* his death. He wrote Trina this with some trepidation. He confessed he didn't have the time or "psychic surplus" to get into a dispute with her. He had to beat out a lot of recently retired poets who could now write full-time and were, therefore, a serious threat to his hopes for the Pulitzer. Encumbered as he was with the crippled syntax of post-adolescent, hormone-driven poetry aspirants, not to mention his potentially bad heart, he was lucky to crank out an occasional chapbook. Could he buy back her supposed rights to one-fourth of his literary empire? If so, how much would she take?

The Baron felt beleaguered, persecuted, invaded by malignant and remorseless spirits. Yet, as he surveyed his motley troops, he felt oddly companioned. A courier, looking much like Greenhill, his feet bound with woolen mufflers, approached to present the news: 32,765 cadavers of horses burning on the fields of Borodino. He had counted every one, so great was his disbelief. This apparition was followed swiftly by a late image of Napoleon astride the little horse named Hope trotting gallantly along the goat paths of Saint Helena. The Emperor had just arrived on the island and rescue still loomed falsely.

"The Soul has Bandaged Moments," the Baron mused mysteriously to his students.

•

HE DROVE Betina to the airport restaurant for lunch. It was attached to a mostly vacant, but, he'd been assured, comfortable hotel. They sat in a booth overlooking a vast flat tract of industrial properties bounded by high chain-link fencing. They regarded this succession of window-less warehouses, the contents of which would remain an eternal secret, as others might have surveyed the holdings of a great and prosperous estate. They dined sumptuously, but quickly. Then he led her down the carpeted corridor off the restaurant to Room III and turned the key. *He knew no haste,* he thought, as he arranged her on the flowered coverlet. *Slowly, slowly up Mount Fujiyama.*

•

"GREENHILL!" the Baron thundered. "Would you ever stop writing like some third sex to some fourth sex and just get down to it, son!"—for he'd felt very tender of late toward his only male student, no matter that he still grinned like an altitude-starved initiate of the Furies. He took Greenhill aside after class and slipped him a box of ribbed, gold-colored condoms: "Greenhill, get out there and tumble."

•

BETINA'S poems had begun to devise configurations in which her female voices bested their arrogant male persecutors. She wrote mythically and powerfully. A disquieting but compliant hero appeared whose aroma was of "cypress and coffee," and who, "like a spoiled horse, fresh from the stable," kept carrying her *to bed. To bed.*

THE BARON would likely have reigned on happily forever had it not been for Greenhill's spiking his cranberry juice at a student-faculty party. The Baron became a wild man. Imitating the dog in Ferlinghetti's poem trotting "freely thru the street," he got down on all fours and sloshed cranberry juice obscenely onto the ankles of the very colleague who'd put down his waterfall. Burney Falls indeed! He then stood on the hostess's sofa and recited the penultimate lines of Anne Sexton's "Consorting with Angels" in a strident, apocalyptic voice:

> *I'm all one skin like a fish.*
> *I'm no more a woman*
> *than Christ was a man.*

Next, as if to exalt by example, the Baron began to strip off his clothes before the horrified gathering. Only Betina, rushing forward with her raincoat, saved him from complete and utter ruin at the hands of the ungrateful mob.

"Greenhill!" he shouted, lunging unsuccessfully for the boy. "Become a medical doctor. Consult livers and spleens. Go into sanitation. Catalog rare fungi in the rain forest. But leave poetry, for God's sake, to the passionate and inspired, you lusterless bog of inertia!" In this last plea he heard his own voice rebound like a runaway droshky, heading straight for him.

With that, the Baron passed out and had to be carried from the house, an immense personage borne away on the shoulders of his obscure and unworthy subjects.

•

THE NEXT morning his wife's tear-stained face seemed inordinately magnified by his feeling of having been bodily occupied by unholy forces who had squandered him in some cruel and futile campaign. It was painful to lift his eyelids. He smelled as if he'd been rubbed head to foot in *Eau de Cologne of Whiskey*. And what of his legacy? What of his one and only voice among the many?

Just like the French, not to bury their dead until the stench compelled them. But here he was, above ground and seemingly alive. True, his standard had been trampled. The Queen of Beauty had retreated through a sea of slippery mud in her closed carriage. Now a turbaned emir in the form of his dear wife approached his bedside with what he took for a sign of treaty, or was it *entreaty*?

"Whose raincoat is this?" he heard the Baroness inquire. The Great Amnesiac raised himself painfully to his elbow and stared at the strange limp artifact. Could this be the dark-blue cloak of Marengo, still damp with sprinkles of holy water? Staring at it, he reflected that it was eminently unfair that the already-bloodied horses of the Polish lancers would yet again have to swim through "knife-edged slabs of ice" to save Napoleon's bacon. And poor Empress Marie Louise—the affront of Marie Walewska's blue-eyed child sired by the Emperor—it was beyond disheartening. Life and history were, he conceded, fraught with intimate betrayals, despotic interludes, impoverished duchies, evacuations by night, twinkling stars over the fugitives, and someone advancing, shouting, "The Cossacks! The Cossacks!"

The Baron reached out and touched the hem of the raincoat. His fingertips reverberated with the current of his unremembered actions from the night before. Indeed an entire tracery of misused power and conscienceless defilement coursed through his being. The snowy escarpment of a singular remorse enfolded him. In his heart's eye he saw a few lonely campfires lit at the foot of a hill.

Or had the torch been put to the imperial carriages? He thought he could smell the Emperor's table linen burning. No matter, he would call for his sheepskin and go forth on foot to dismantle the shabby impostors who had been wreaking such havoc in his kingdom. When he returned, he would see to it that the horse named King George henceforth would be called *Sheikh*. He must, if he survived, interrogate the pastry cook about how to make the oranges sweeter.

The Baron hoped, should anything befall him, the little hair he had left would be sufficient to provide ringlets for his beloved family members. His students would be glad for any remaining snippets. Faintly, at the back of his cranium, he could hear the relic-seekers at Longwood ripping the Chinese wallpaper away like the frenzied rats who'd enlivened the floorboards under the Emperor's dinner table.

He turned at the door and embraced the Baroness as if he might never see her again, for he did love her dearly. And, at that moment, as he later would distantly recount, "big tears began to fall from his eyes."

One memorable tiff involved Bertha the Adder and Seattle Emily. Bertha was so incensed that she tore off all Emily's clothes in the brawl on the riverfront, then chased her through town, pelting her naked hide with rocks.

The
Woman
Who
Prayed

Dotty Lloyd believed herself happily married to a
rural mailman named Del—until she came across a
cache of love letters from Hilda Queener. It so happened,
only the day before, Hilda's poodle had become overex-
cited and piddled all over the waiting-room couch at the
Lady Fox Pet Boutique where Dotty worked.

The instant Dotty discovered Hilda had penned the
hidden letters, a memory of a distasteful childhood
encounter sprang to mind. Hilda, the daughter of a den-
tist, had carried herself in junior high with the cool poise
of a giraffe at a kite convention. She smelled of Jergens
lotion and she was fond of cherry-flavored Life Savers
which she shared with her friends. Dotty's father owned
and operated the only pest-control service in the town.

She gave off the pungent odor of chemicals designed to eradicate.

Nearly thirty years had passed since the two had tangled in eighth grade over Roger Gillwater. Hilda, with great gusto, had slapped Dotty's face in front of their class because Roger had dared to walk Dotty home. In Hilda's mind, Roger was reserved for Hilda. Luckily for him, after high school he'd migrated to Hawaii, where he married a part owner of a beach-side hotel. He had appeared the previous year at their twenty-fifth class reunion wearing leis of lavender orchids and had twice excused himself from his wife to dance with Dotty. On their second foray onto the dance floor, Hilda floated by on a slow number with a grade school principal, and reached over playfully to pick a blossom from one of the leis around Roger's neck. Then the principal's shoulder carried away her knowing smile.

As Dotty now turned one of the letters in her hands, Hilda's jealous slap lashed her cheek across time and space like a one-winged bird. There in the garage, the stunned faces of her adolescent classmates came back to her. They seemed to lean with her over her unfortunate find. The letters had been mailed to Del at P.O. Box 1422. "Queenie," they were signed. "Love, Queenie." Dotty began to check their postmarks to determine the extent and timing of her husband's betrayal. She assumed this was the feared midlife crisis that caused a man in his forties to veer off in search of the "absolute cheese," as one of her customers had put it.

It was scalding in those initial moments to note that the letters had been carefully arranged in the order Del had received them. She saw with chagrin that the top one was dated only three days earlier. Furthermore, the correspondence spanned an entire year and each month's bundle was secured with a wide rubber band, the kind Del used on his mail route. Clearly the letters had been treasured.

She might never have come across them if she hadn't made that foray into the garage to the paint and polish shelves. Dotty had decided to resurrect a scuffed ivory purse for the spring wedding of a niece, and the cardboard box marked "Smoke Detector" had attracted her attention.

Her initial shock was followed quickly by outrage. She fell upon the contents like a lioness onto the carcass of an antelope on the wide Serengeti. She carried the box into the bicycle shed at the back of the house and plugged in an electric heater to ward off the spring damp. After securing the foot stand on her bicycle, she climbed onto the seat to be closer to the lightbulb. There she began to read. Her eyes and heart moved through the pages— hours and days of events of which she'd known nothing.

"My darling, Del,"—the letters often began. Dotty never addressed Del as her "darling." It was a word she considered definitely over the mark. Though they'd been passionate in their twenties, they'd developed a kindly, affectionate intimacy over the years. Sweetie she called him, and Sugar. He called her Pumpkin.

She pored through the contents of the letters. The light of the bare electric bulb emphasized the surreptitious nature of her inquiry. "Oh Del, I can hardly bear to know you are so close, yet so far." The expressions, though sickeningly pitched at the level of soap opera, still had the power to wring her heart. Weren't these the very things illicit lovers *always* said?

After the ache died back, though, Hilda's spasmodically expressed longing for Del strangely began to relieve Dotty. She considered it evidence of her husband's care in not meeting her childhood rival too often. He clearly did not want to arouse suspicion and bring on the collapse of their marriage. Or was she grasping at straws? No sooner had she been able to shore herself up than she would read from Hilda: "Your letters are a great comfort to me." Just to imagine love letters from Del, nestled among lingerie from Frederick's of Hollywood in Hilda's bureau across town, made Dotty fairly steam. She and Del had courted beginning in high school, so they hadn't needed love letters. She felt retroactively robbed! She wanted to drive to Hilda's with a box of matches and a barrel of kerosene.

Instead, she took the letters from the box, hid them under a sack of birdseed, and unplugged the heater. Then she returned the box to the garage shelf and made straight for the beach down the hill. It was Wednesday, her one afternoon off. She needed to get hold of herself before Del came home at five.

Like the ocean before her, Dotty's mind began to move in and out over her dilemma. She noticed that the ocean no longer consoled her. It instead presented itself as a huge methodical system which mulled and combed and splashed itself from time to time. It simply claimed, then retracted; mulled, then recoiled. With the tide frothing toward the white logs marooned on the beach, she made the decision not to confront Del with what she'd found until she was ready.

Somehow she got through the evening without bursting into tears or saying anything sharp or insinuating to Del. They watched a program on an archaeological dig somewhere in the Middle East, had a snack of cantaloupe, and went to bed. Lying next to Del, knowing about the letters, caused her to feel more alone than she could recall. She turned away from him, drawing her knees up inside her gown. Just as she dropped into sleep,

Hilda Queener whirled past with one of Roger Gill-water's leis garlanding her long neck.

At her job next morning, a feeling of counterfeit normalcy returned. She ran shears over Bucky, a black cocker spaniel, and considered how to bring up the subject of the letters to Del. She feared she would accuse, berate, and condemn. And why not? He had to answer for what he was doing. Yet even to speak of this would involve such a departure from the safe shore of their mutual respect and kindliness that the prospect overwhelmed her. She knew that once she told Del of her discovery, Hilda would take center stage. As long as Dotty kept things to herself, in a way the betrayal hadn't quite happened. The secret of her discovery matched the secret of the affair.

It seemed prophetic that she was working on Bucky as she addressed her quandary. The dog, named after Buckminster Fuller, lay on its side with the plaintive whites of its eyes showing. Bucky had been saved by an architect just prior to his scheduled execution at the pound. Dotty ran the electric clippers carefully along one black velvet ear cradled over her palm. When she stared into those brown eyes she thought she glimpsed a kindred soul. The animal seemed to beseech, to ask perpetually to be spared. She wanted as much.

That night after dinner their church fellowship group arrived at the house for their scheduled "visiting night." After reading and discussing Scripture together, it was customary, at the end of such visits, to ask the householders if they would like to discuss any personal trouble. Dotty felt herself trembling when Ms. Carriveau, the feisty group leader, asked, "Now, is there anything we can do for *you?*" Dotty looked toward Del, but his head was already bowed in preparation for the closing words. They all joined hands and Ginger Carriveau gave a blanket, all-purpose prayer. Dotty was grateful to shut her eyes and bow her own head, not to have to look at Del, who showed not a trace of remorse or guilt.

Inside the calm space of prayer, Dotty felt comforted. She'd always prayed at the usual times and places. But this time the benevolent, concentrated force she'd been closing her eyes toward since childhood seemed to have been patiently awaiting her. As she prayed now, in the secret pain of her discovery, the letters seemed to shed some of their power, to recede from the infectious claim they'd begun to make on her life.

"May you, Del and Dotty, trust in each other, and in God's will. Let His guidance come into your hearts. Amen," Ginger said confidently, as if, by expressing this aloud, it was sure to happen. They continued in silence for a few moments, as was their custom, offering their private prayers. Del's palm clasped Dotty's in seemingly perfect agreement to their life together. How dear he was, despite all. It was hard to believe he could be apart from her, straying with the likes of the twice-divorced Hilda Queener.

After the members of the fellowship group shook hands and headed to their cars, Dotty turned and gazed at Del. He had the untarnished look of a pilgrim in frontier portraits of the first Thanksgiving. His mild blue eyes, set deeply below his high forehead, belied her recent discovery.

During the rest of the evening they were tender with each other and she had the strong impulse to reveal that she'd found the letters. But the urge gave way to wanting to visit the letters once again, alone. Inside the prayer, Dotty had been able to feel *she,* not the letters, held the power. The fact that she could let this trouble drift offshore for a time, without addressing it, gave her hope that her relationship with Del was durable, resilient enough to withstand whatever might come. Even this. There was no reason to hurry. That had been the lasting message of the waves as she'd walked the day before.

Later that night, while Del was showering, she decided to make a trip to the bicycle shed. She picked up a box of wooden matches from the counter and took a saucepan from the cupboard. Once inside the shed, she put the pan and matches down, took up one of the recent letters and climbed, like a schoolgirl, onto the unsteady perch of her bicycle. She read the letter in its entirety. Hilda Queener provided the sorts of details she could not banish—that she wore Del's flannel shirt to bed, a shirt he'd left with her for that purpose. Hilda wrote she was "putting aside a little spare cash" for them "to take a cozy holiday together." Dotty nearly flew apart at the word "cozy." The last holiday she and Del had taken, the previous summer, they'd pulled their camper near LaPush, sixty miles west, and parked in a clear-cut overlooking the ocean. Dotty read on, bracing herself. Hilda said she was keeping the money in a jar under the sink. "When can you get away?" she asked—as if Del were held prisoner in his own home!

Dotty stepped down from the bicycle and picked up the box of matches. She took one out and ran it along the pebbled side of the box until the head snapped and darted into flame. As she knelt over the saucepan, she took up the letter and held the match to it. In the relative darkness of the windowless shed the letter, with Hilda's handwriting across its pages, caught fire and seemed to rush upward, assuming heat and power in the small space. The eagerness of the love letter to burn caused her to open her mouth like a child before summer bonfires at the beach. Was she imagining it, or did the pages seem more

225

free, more ardent as they burned? She held page after page of the letter as it lifted into the dark. She hated the letter's agreement to its destruction, its lack of shame. "The hussy!" she said, and heard her mother's voice echo inside her own, as she'd castigated women who "shacked up" rather than marry.

The final bits of paper, tinged with blue, dropped into the saucepan where they smoldered and blackened. She felt mixed about what she'd done. It seemed entirely within her rights, yet, at the same time, she knew it was a weakness to have gone so far. She recalled a story from one of her customers, the owner of a German shepherd with hip trouble. This woman had discovered a single love letter hidden in her husband's fishing-tackle box, next to a Blue Devil lure. She'd waited until he was in the shower to confront him. Then she'd insisted he stay buck-naked, water trickling down his body like sweat, and burn the letter over the toilet, in front of her, to prove that, as he insisted, the woman meant nothing to him. *This,* Dotty had felt, was going too far.

She glanced at the remaining packets. They defied her to consign them to ashes and, for the time being, won a reprieve. She picked up the saucepan and matches and started to the house, pausing to knock the ashes into the brambles.

It was quiet in the house as she entered. She turned the deadbolt and saw that the lights were off in the den. Del had evidently gone to bed. She sat down in the darkened living room and gazed into the yard, lit only by their neighbor's house lights. She had come a long way from the relief and comfort of the prayer earlier that evening. She smelled of smoke, of hidden love, of secrets and betrayal.

The next morning after Del left for the post office she

walked out into their yard in her bathrobe. She was working afternoons the rest of the week and she was glad for time alone. At the base of the apple tree she noticed the faint green-yellow buds of daffodils pursed on the verge of opening. A wren was splashing in the hanging birdbath of the Japanese plum. The scene was guileless, bathed in sunlight. Like a stranger to her own life, she stood in their yard with bounty all around her, and allowed herself a strange impulse. She bowed her head. After a few moments with her eyes closed she felt she'd stepped outside time. Her spirit reeled forth into a vastness that had been there all the time, but which she approached now out of her own direct need. Her attention seemed sturdy and calculated to let any attending powers know she appreciated all she'd been given, despite this recent trouble. She gave thanks for the assurance beauty itself was in the world—that there was a vibrant stir of aliveness of which she was a part, however small.

When she opened her eyes, she saw her home with Del afresh—the swing set they'd painted together, the mailbox with their names: "Del and Dot Lloyd" lettered in gold and black, the hummingbird feeder wired to a post near the red-currant bush where the birds would be sure to find it when they returned from their winter migration.

Her uplift in spirit caused her to recall something their pastor had said recently in a sermon: "Prayer is a way of spreading God's presence. As Paul said, 'Pray without ceasing.'" So, perhaps it followed that the more a person prayed, the more God would indeed exist in the world. And the more of God there was in the world, the more banished would be the likes of Hilda Queener—for she knew from living in the same town all these years that Hilda's amorous exertions had caused more than one marriage to ricochet out of orbit. Prayer or no prayer, she couldn't get Hilda out of the picture.

For the next several nights she burned letters over the saucepan. When the last one had crumbled into a gray ash, she realized she knew something she couldn't have known any other way. She hadn't changed anything between Del and Hilda, or between Del and herself, but she had fruitfully crossed and recrossed the boundary between outright anger and aching dismay. Pain had a way of cauterizing itself, she knew, if you could stand it, or stand up to it.

She began to pray in odd moments during her days at the Lady Fox as she groomed a steady succession of animals. She knew it was wrong to ask for things out of selfish motives, but she brazened away, inwardly, and asked that Hilda Queener suffer some debilitation. Nothing life-threatening, mind you. Only purely cosmetic manifestations, such as the sudden release of foul odors, or perhaps if her gums could show when she laughed, or a craving for raw garlic might overtake her. Then Dotty quickly tried to make up for this by praying for refugees in war-torn corners of the world.

After grooming two paired Pekingese and later an Afghan, she went for a break in the little outside snack area. But the prayers wouldn't stop coming. She bowed her head for Hillary Rodham Clinton, who'd been relentlessly under attack. Then she prayed for Robert Dole's crippled arm, his hand carrying the pen with which he would never write illicitly, she felt sure, to any woman across town, or even across the nation, for that matter. She tossed in Newt Gingrich out of concern for what she assumed an apoplectic disposition. Since she was herself a Democrat and a woman, she doubted God's investment in the current ascendant breed of Republican—though, as with other wayward souls, she assumed the heavenly door might be left ajar for them to repent and be brought into the fold at some later time. She offered these political prayers in good faith, knowing they might do no more than ripple the surface of her own soul as they wafted off into the universe. But wasn't this the sure good of prayer, that it boomeranged back toward the one who prayed and gave a modicum of hope?

Dotty's boss, Julie, came outside to smoke and found her standing under the maple with her eyes closed.

"Just taking some sun," Dotty said, and did not open her eyes. Julie puffed on her cigarette in silence for a while downwind of Dotty, making curt little snapping noises when her lips left the cigarette. The smoke had a heady, narcotic effect, reminding Dotty of the charred but mentally resilient love letters.

"My hands are itching like crazy," Julie said. "I swear that shampoo leaks right through my rubber gloves!" she complained.

"Uh-huh," Dotty said, and kept on with her prayer for the owner of the Afghan, Cara Jensen, who'd just been told she was out of remission on her breast cancer. Cara had long ago told Dotty that her name in Italian meant "dear one." "Take care, dear Lord, of your dear one, Cara," Dotty prayed.

After Julie went inside, Dotty gave a prayer for Julie's red, chemically scalded hands, so like her own. Then she moved quickly to ask for blessings on a dog named Zowie she'd read about in the morning paper. The animal had been shot and killed protecting its master's home from intruders. She didn't want to neglect this innocent, sacrificed in the line of duty. Its homebound fate was somehow very moving to her.

That night Dotty was gazing out the window as Del

drove his pickup into the garage. She heard the truck door slam, but he did not enter the house immediately. She thought of the empty box on the shelf and wondered if he was going to it now, intending to add yet another letter from Hilda, but discovering the others missing.

These thoughts accompanied her present endeavor to keep her mind inside a stream of prayerful reverie she'd entered near the end of her shift at the Lady Fox. She had begun to pray with her eyes open. This allowed her continuous access to her prayers. Dotty had offered so many prayers that day that, if her efforts counted for anything, she was convinced God must be more amply present in the world. Certainly she felt deeply infused by her own attentiveness to those for whom she prayed.

When Del came into the house he said nothing to indicate any change, and they set about fixing a little dinner together of spaghetti and fresh salad. He behaved in a very deferential way to Dotty, as if trying to make something up to her, without revealing what it was. If he had discovered the letters missing, he also had chosen silence.

That night Dotty prayed in the shower and while brushing her teeth—for the sound of running water acted as a natural stimulant to prayer. The longer she kept the secret of the letters, the more the scope of her prayerfulness widened. Virtually every waking moment was spent addressing herself to her prayers. They allowed her to lift away from Del's affair, to bypass it, to ward it off with a genuine and specific concern for others.

As soon as she'd completed one prayer, another suggested itself. She realized how busy the nuns and monks must have been for centuries in their monasteries. She had clearly underestimated them. Each day, when her customers told her of this or that calamity, she set to work. She kept God busy. *She* was busy.

That night in bed, trying to move into sleep, she continued to pray, as if all would be lost if she ceased to perform her repeated pleas. When she tried to regard her effort as possibly hopeless—a silly waste of time—something strong and resilient flared up against her doubt. Del was turned on his side, away from her, but she was aware of his sleeping head on the pillow next to hers. Possibly filled with dreams of Hilda. She couldn't know. For her own part she lay throughout the night in a prayerful drowse that carried her into morning.

When she got out of bed and went downstairs, she saw that Del had already left for work. She was struck by his having gone from the house without waking her. This was unlike him, and unlike her not to have woken. She recalled the moment from past mornings when, after breakfasting together, they kissed good-bye at the door, that island of once harmless departure which had become so bittersweet of late. She saw that his lunch box was missing and that the mayonnaise had been left with its lid off where he'd made his sandwiches. Why this should have caused her to tremble and move toward tears, she didn't know. When she finally quieted herself, she had the urge to pray for something momentous—for Lebanese refugees, for the bereaved relatives of airline passengers lost in a Florida swamp; for anyone, anywhere betrayed, bereft, and lonely. She lit a votive candle on a side table near the couch in the living room and got down before it on her knees.

In some paralysis of her own needs, she focused on the fate of her marriage and on her love for Del. Treacherous or not, he was still her husband, and she'd made all kinds of allowances for him because of what she knew of the wiles of Hilda Queener. She closed her eyes and entered a long, narrow corridor of necessity. She was praying for herself. She was unsure, as with the whole idea of prayer, whether or not her effort was wasted. God could fail to hear or to answer. She might lose her husband to Hilda. But there was something worse than losing Del. She might plunge into a life of doubt and bitter inward-gazing while she raked her soul hopelessly across the unbroken silence of God.

The world felt more intimate there on her knees. The candle flickered and dodged across her face in the day-light. After a while she relaxed into her own love letter, a prayer which issued from her as naturally and needfully as breath. It was intoxicating, like the smell of seaweed—tidal and vast, going out across the planet, touching all, pleading for all.

Prayer unceasing kept her on her knees until the dark came down. It was late when Del returned home. She was aware when he parked in the garage and entered the silent house. A door closed as he crossed into the adjoining room on his way to her. Finally he was over her and she felt him lifting her from her knees by one arm. Then his voice, low and halting, from a distance, as he began to try to explain.

CREDITS

Excerpts from *Saloons of the Old West* by Richard Erdoes (New York: Alfred A. Knopf, 1979). Reprinted by permission of Alfred A. Knopf.

Excerpts from *Hummingbirds: Their Life and Behavior*, text by Esther Quesada Tyrrel, photographs by Robert A. Tyrrell (New York: Crown Publishers, 1985). Reprinted by permission of Crown.

Excerpt from *Whiskey and Wild Women: An Amusing Account of the Saloons and Bawds of the Old West* by Cy Martin (New York: Hart Publishing Company, 1974).